Mourning into Dancing: A Journey into the Soul

AARON PETTES

ELK LAKE PUBLISHING INC®

PUBLISHING THE POSITIVE
Plymouth, Massachusetts

A Christian Company

COPYRIGHT NOTICE

Cover and Interior Design: Derinda Babcock

Editor(s): Mary W. Johnson, Cristel Phelps, Deb Haggerty

PUBLISHED BY: Elk Lake Publishing, Inc., 35 Dogwood Drive, Plymouth, MA 02360, 2021

Library Cataloging Data

Names: Pettes, Aaron (Aaron Pettes)

Mourning into Dancing: A Journey into the Soul / Aaron Pettes

218 p. 23cm × 15cm (9in × 6 in.)

ISBN-13: 978-1-64949-473-3 (paperback) | 978-1-64949-474-0 (trade paperback) | 978-1-64949-475-7 (e-book)

Key Words: speculative, inspirational, Christian, short story format, philosophical, salvation, life of the soul

Library of Congress Control Number: 2021953497 Fiction

DEDICATION

To Pamela Ann,
Dream of me
I will be there waiting
It's the only way.
But only for now,
Their time will end
Ours will begin.
This book is for you.

TABLE OF CONTENTS

ACKNOWLEDGMENTS

This book was, of course, a work of God's grace in my life. First and foremost, he gets credit.

Secondly, the team at Elk Lake. Deb Haggerty, thank you for giving me continued support, and to the Tinkerers, Mary Johnson and Cristel Phelps, thank you for your concerted efforts. I am blessed by this team.

To my family, all the same love and devotion. Y'all know how I feel and how much you mean to me. But a special word goes out to the love of my life, Pamela Ann. Without you in my life, I would have so much less joy. It is an honor that God gave me the blessing of you in my life.

Eagles Nest in Omaha, my God-given family ... keep doing what you do because your belief in the saved sinner and the potential they hold is transformative. I am a product of you. Stand tall.

PREFACE

Hello!

Thank you for picking up this book and beginning this journey with me. I sit in a unique position in life. I am afforded many hours of self-reflection that most in this busy world don't receive. You see, I'm in prison. I was convicted of crimes that led me to this place of self-reflection, and during that time I was convicted by the Holy Spirit. At that very moment, my story changed, and the stories that follow began. Jesus Christ has taken "the least of these" and transformed everything in my life. For fifteen years, he has molded me, and I am blessed to have been used by him.

When I sat down to write this book, I wanted to put together a group of stories that talk about the things we as Christians usually avoid. I wanted to start a conversation with you, my reader. If along the way you laugh or cry, then I've done my job. Better yet, if they cause you to reflect, then I praise God. The stories do not necessarily propose answers to any of the questions they raise, or judgment on any of the positions they pose. They are merely fodder for thought about pain, grief, love, fear, confusion, anger—all emotions and concepts that most Christians wrestle with on a regular basis, and none of which negate our faith's veracity. Hopefully, they serve to deepen it.

A quick note on the placement of "The Butterfly Trilogy." I wrote this story over nearly a decade. Inside this book, the content appears organically, as it did in my life. The arrangement is appropriate, as intimate love isn't a lesson one learns in a single sitting but throughout one's journey through life, much to our heartache. If love's entanglements and redeeming nature could be gleaned as quickly as turning a page, we'd all be saved much struggle, but then we'd also lose most of its potential.

I hope you enjoy *Mourning into Dancing*, and that it blesses you. Laugh. Cry. Agree. Disagree. Grieve. Rejoice. Do it all! But above all, give thanks to God because it is he who has made this world so uniquely diverse that we all experience it so differently, yet so similarly.

The journey ... it's all about the journey.

CHAPTER 1

BUTTERFLY TRILOGY, PART 1: THE OASIS

The hot sun blazed in the sky, its rays falling onto the earth and scorching everything they touched. The man plowed doggedly through the dunes of the desert wasteland, the hot sands sapping his energy as they burned the soles of his bare feet. His clothes had long since shredded to tatters and hung loosely from his dark bronzed skin, and yet he continued toward a forgotten goal.

The only thing that kept him going now was the idea of water. How long had it been since he had felt the cool liquid on his burned palate? Hours? Days? A week? He could barely remember his name, let alone say when last his parched throat and heart had found relief. *One foot in front of the other.* That had been his mantra for too long.

Now, as his left foot struck the burning sand, his knee buckled, and he tumbled down the steep slope in a tangle of limbs. The ungraceful spiral was agony as the sand made contact with his skin. He spread-eagled at the bottom of the dune on his back, with no energy to pull his burning body from the desert's unforgiving surface.

He stared and screamed at his fiery companion shining high in the clear blue sky.

"You win!" He closed his eyes to the sun's penetrating rays, resigning himself to whatever ending lay ahead of him.

Much time passed before he opened his eyes again, but the sun was still high overhead. He wondered how much longer it would be before his desert journey would be over. Not long now, he was sure.

DANCINGDANCINGDANCING.

A shadow passed in front of his tired eyes, and he squinted, trying to make out what had cast it. Were those wings?

Yes, those were definitely wings. Not the wings of a bird. These fluttered back and forth through the air, and like a kite on a string, they bounced on the air currents heading directly toward him. With no energy left to defend himself, he had no choice but to watch the apparition descend straight at his head.

When it fluttered a few feet away, he scrunched up his face and awaited the impact of the creature who had surely come to feed upon his supine form. When contact was made, there was no pain, only the light tickle of six tiny feet alighting upon his nose. He stifled a sneeze and opened his eyes.

What he found was a small butterfly looking back at him with shiny black eyes. Its wings were colored in brilliant hues, changing constantly from one color to another. Pink darkened into purple, which morphed into blue, then shaded to green and then blazing yellow. The creature was like nothing he'd ever seen, so mesmerizing it was.

Why would a butterfly be in the depths of this inferno? But no sooner had he thought it, he decided he didn't care. This was the most beautiful thing he had ever seen, and if this dry place was where his journey ended, he'd be happy to look upon this creature until his last moment.

The butterfly took two tiny steps up the bridge of his nose and appeared to look right into him, as if asking him a question. He found himself speaking in a cracked whisper.

"Hello, little one," he said. The tiny head cocked to the other side as if in response to the statement.

"I wish we could fly away together," the man said painfully. The butterfly rose into the air for a few seconds, and the man froze, afraid of losing his new friend. His fear subsided as the butterfly landed again on the bridge of his nose, and once again, he stifled a sneeze.

"A little rest," he spoke to his new companion and then closed his eyes blearily. As he did, soft sounds carried on the desert air—a musical sound, like wind chimes, and when he focused on the butterfly on his nose, a shimmer surrounded it. With no more energy to spare, he closed his eyes.

A few seconds passed and he was sure the music was louder now, almost upon him. He heard a voice.

"Open your eyes." The voice was like silk across his skin. "Come now, you must open your eyes."

The man obeyed, and when he did, everything was different.

He looked around in disbelief, struggling to make sense of what he saw. He stood in an oasis. Gone were the hot sands and the baking sun, replaced by lush green grass, tall leafy trees with songbirds flitting from branch to branch, and a cool sun in the sky. He looked up to feel the soft warmth of the sun's caress on his face, instead of the usual searing heat.

His gaze came back earthward, and he saw to his right the shimmering blue waters of a pond. The heart in his chest began to gallop, and with a burst of speed he didn't know he still possessed, he sprinted to the pond. His only thought was to feel the water on his skin.

When he reached the bank, he dove in heedlessly. He sank to the silty bottom, and holding his breath, opened his eyes to look up. The sun above lit the pond, but he had no urge at that moment to return to the surface. Letting the water hold him below, he saw a shadow pass across the surface above. It seemed to beckon him back up. Then he remembered his companion, the butterfly.

He pushed off the bottom and rocketed up, breaking the surface with a shout. Trudging up the bank, he found his clothes were no longer rags, but whole again, and dry as if they had never been wet. His skin, too, was completely dry.

"What is this place?"

Standing in the lush grass on the bank of the pond, he heard a soft rustle to his left. He turned, expecting to see a butterfly floating on the air. Instead, there was a sight more mystifying than the previous creature, more beautiful by far.

A woman like none he'd ever seen before stood not far away. She was no taller than his chin, her hair seemed in constant motion, although there was no wind. Her simple, flowing dress fell to her knees. Translucent and yet not, its color changed as it drifted around her body. The smile on her beautiful face shone like the moon on the darkest night, riveting him where he stood. But her eyes ... her eyes were the most amazing things he'd ever seen. They were blue one moment, green the next, then brown, then hazel. They examined him with piercing interest.

She skipped to him with brazen courage and stopped close enough that he had to look down at her. This near, she was even more gut-wrenchingly lovely, and his breath caught in his chest.

"Hello," she said with a musical quality. "How do you feel?"

"Good," he choked out. "Is this real?"

Giggling, she stepped forward, their bodies almost touching now.

"Of course, it is," she replied archly. She stood there watching him daringly as his heart beat wildly in his chest.

He didn't know where the sudden burst of courage came from, but he couldn't stop himself from stooping low and kissing her softly on her lips. He quickly pulled away, embarrassed by his audacity. He found her looking at him with a puzzled smile on her sweet face.

"I ... I'm sorry," he stammered.

A gleeful chuckle burst from his chest then, belying his words. In that moment, a last renegade droplet of water shook free from his hair and landed on his nose, and a sudden series of sneezes wracked his frame. He closed his eyes as tears of irritation flowed. It lasted only a few seconds, but when he opened his eyes again, he was back in the desert, lying on his back in the baking sun, staring up into its searing gaze.

He lay for a second in complete despair. He closed his eyes and opened them again, finding himself still firmly planted in the desert. He saw no green grass, no songbirds, no cooling pond, no beautiful woman. Only sand, blasted sand. He let out a shout of heartbreak, expecting his scorched vocal cords to snap at the strain.

Only they didn't. They held true, and his voice roared across the dunes. It was then he noticed the change. His skin no longer ached with steady pain. Wiggling his toes without agony was something incomprehensible only a short while ago, but now felt normal. He licked his lips to find no cracks or blisters there. His tongue was its usual size, the swelling of dehydration gone. He just felt *good*.

He rolled over and stood up, a revitalizing energy humming through his body. He could continue his journey now. *One foot in front of the other*, he said to himself as he started to walk back up the dune he had tumbled down.

Where had he gone? Was it real? He didn't know the answer to the first question, but he did on the second one. Yes, it was real. The proof of it was evident in his healed body and mended spirit. As he mused over his thoughts a shadow passed over him, and he looked up to see a streak

7

of color flitting to the top of the dune and hovering there. Waiting.

He laughed in joy as he continued to the top of the hill of sand and the floating butterfly. Musical notes floated on the desert air.

"Hello to you too," the man chuckled as he reached the top. The butterfly landed on his ear, chiming its music.

What lay beyond the next dune? Where exactly was he going? He still didn't know for sure, but with his new strength and colorful partner ... he knew he'd make it.

TO BE CONTINUED ...

CHAPTER 2

SOMETIMES ... TOWERS FALL

PAIN AND POSSIBILITY

"Is it possible to change the mind of God?" the fifty-two-year-old man asked his dying daughter. "Once his decision has been made, can we alter the course he's set?"

Francis Neagley spoke to his daughter as though she'd sit up in her hospital bed at any moment and respond. He'd been at his vigil for ten days now, and with each passing minute, the likelihood of her recovery grew less. The slimmer the possibility became, the more he spoke. It was a connection, to his daughter and to reality. Without the conversation, his grief threatened to swamp his heart and drown him in sorrow. So he spoke, for himself and for his daughter.

"Inoperable brain tumor," he continued. "What is that to God? A God who created everything we can see can surely handle a brain tumor. You're only thirty years old."

His breath caught in his lungs. *Too young. This must be a mistake. How can I change God's mind?*

Francis laid his head down on the side of the hospital bed and wept, one hand holding his daughter's limp hand and the other balled in the sheets. He cried until he was out of tears and then raised his head and looked at his little girl.

"Beautiful," he said. "You're so beautiful."

She was, in fact, withered and frail. In the ten days since she'd been admitted, she'd lost twenty pounds, and her complexion was haggard and gray. Her father saw none of that. He saw his daughter, his little girl, and he couldn't see anything more.

"Do you remember the time we went to Chuck E. Cheese Pizza & Arcade for your birthday? You were seven, I think." He waited for her response and didn't seem to notice that he got none.

"You were so happy. All your mother and I heard for months in advance was, 'Can we go to Chuck Cheez's for my birthday?' You couldn't even get the name right. It was adorable. And then when we told you we were going the week before," he chuckled at the memory, "I thought you'd explode from the pure joy of the moment. The next week was torture for your mom and me. 'Will Chuck Cheez sing 'Happy Birthday' to me? Do you think Chuck Cheez knows we're coming? How many games can I play at Chuck Cheez's?'

"And on and on. How can one little girl come up with so many questions? Then when we got there ... you were enthralled. The look on your face when you walked in was the epitome of childlike wonder. We played so many games, ate too much pizza, and then the robot Chuck E. Cheese sang 'Happy Birthday' to you. I never thought a kid could be as happy as you were.

"You told me when we were done eating that it was the best birthday ever ... and it was, for our whole family. Me, your mom, and you, all together."

Francis Neagley grew quiet as he reminisced.

"We left the restaurant, and as we were leaving, there was a bag lady asleep outside the building. I wouldn't have even noticed her if you hadn't stopped walking. You stood there holding the Chuck E. Cheese stuffed animal we bought for you that night, and you looked at her. The expression on your face was of such concern. It was your day, and in the midst of it you saw this broken, homeless woman. You noticed.

"'Daddy,' you asked, 'can I give her my Chuck Cheez?'"

He smiled to himself. "Your mother and I looked at each other with pride and love because with that question we knew ... we knew we were raising you right.

"Your mom said, 'Of course, baby,' and you walked right up to the sleeping woman and tucked your Chuck E. Cheese into the sleeping woman's arms. The woman didn't even notice as you walked away. You were an amazing person even then."

Francis said her name.

"Sarah." He waited for a response expectantly. "Sarah, can we change the mind of God? All the good we've done, all the prayers we've prayed, all the love we've shared ... it has to count, right?"

The fluorescent light above the hospital bed flickered, the only response Francis Neagley received. He sat and gazed at his daughter's face while listening to the array of machines keeping her alive. The slow wheeze of the ventilator, the annoying yet comforting ping of the heart monitor, the drip of the IV, all the sounds comprised a kind of macabre orchestra of medical instruments. Their somber melody was the only indication of life in his daughter. He listened fervently to their music as he began to speak again.

"I remember when you brought your first boyfriend home." He chuckled softly at the memory. "He was such an obvious loser. I didn't know how to react to him, this clown standing in my living room. With his slicked-back hair, white T-shirt, and ripped jeans, he was something out of a 1960s greaser movie. Such a fool. But you were smitten, and I knew you'd think I was trying to be mean if I scared him off. So, I smiled and shook his hand, then went upstairs into my room and prayed." Another chuckle.

"And when he inevitably broke your heart a few weeks later, I was there to hold you while you cried your sixteen-year-old eyes out. I smoothed your hair, cooed in your ear, and told you how smart and special you were. I said, 'If the butthead can't see that, then he doesn't deserve you,' and it was true. You were so shocked to hear your dad the pastor cuss you immediately broke into a mix of giggles and sobs. Pretty soon we were both laughing hysterically and holding each other. Your mom came in and found us trying to stifle our laughs like two high school girls. At least one of us had an excuse." He took a breath, lost in the memory again. "So long ago. So much ... so long ... since then. Your mother, my faith ... but not you. Please God, not you."

He choked on another sob, and his grip tightened on the sheets as he refused to cry again. He channeled all his grief into his heart, willing himself not to let go. The grief coalesced in his chest and grew in intensity until the white-hot ball of pent-up emotion slowly changed into anger and rage. Francis Neagley could sense the impending eruption and knew if he didn't release some of the pressure, the damage of holding it in would be catastrophic.

"Why?" he hissed at the heavens.

"Why?" he accused.

"You ... *cannot* ... *take her*!" he threatened.

"Not her. Take me!" he begged. "I'll do anything. I'll come back to your flock. Shepherd your sheep, whatever you want. Just tell me, I'll do it." His rage cooled to a simmering anger. "Just tell me."

So lost in the moment was Francis Neagley that he wasn't aware someone else was in the room, until a dry cough sounded behind him. He whipped around to see a doctor standing there in a white lab coat, holding a clipboard. He wore a bemused look on his face and held Francis's eyes until Francis was forced to look away.

"Yes?" Francis asked heatedly, the anger plain in his voice.

The doctor stood there seeming to take pleasure in the naked rage so obvious in the other man.

"I couldn't help but hear your question." The doctor dragged the letter *s* into a hissing sound. "Might I be of assistance?"

Francis Neagley locked eyes with the doctor and felt a chill run down his spine. When he spoke his voiced sounded outside himself, disconnected.

"How can you help me?"

The doctor looked at him hungrily. "Sometimes it's not possible to change the mind of God. But it's *always* possible to make a deal with the devil."

THE INTRODUCTION

Francis gaped at the doctor as he tried to process what had just been said.

"Huh?"

The doctor continued to regard Francis with a burning intensity. He wore a slight smile that didn't seem to match the blasphemous words flowing so easily from his mouth.

"I heard your piteous cries." The words slithered out into the air. "I couldn't help but throw my professional opinion into the conversation." He flattened the lapels of his white lab coat. "You were asking ... threatening ... begging God to spare your daughter. Yes?"

Francis found his voice. "Yes. Yes, I was."

The doctor narrowed his eyes. "Well, I was saying that sometimes it is not possible to change the mind of God, but it *is* possible to make a deal with the devil."

Francis looked at the young man in front of him. He was of average height and weight. His brown skin gave him a Middle Eastern look, and the accent he spoke with was definitely ... foreign. Other than the oddity of his sibilant sounding of the letter *s*, the man before him was unassuming, until Francis looked into his eyes.

As Francis watched, the irises of the doctor's eyes thinned and disappeared as his pupils expanded outward.

The blackness finally filled both his eyes, pushing out even the whites. The black orbs pulsed with supernatural energy, and a howl of primal fear roared in Francis's ears. Cold sweat broke out on his body. The air in his lungs froze, and his exhaled breath formed a frozen plume of air as it passed his lips.

He blinked, and the man standing before him had regular brown eyes and a sarcastic smile, but his cold sweat remained. The memory of the last few moments clawed through his mind. This was no ordinary man standing before him, but an evil creature, more evil than anything on earth.

Francis was surprised he could speak. "So, you're the devil?"

The doctor laughed. "No, Francis, I'm not the devil. I'm a mediator of sorts."

"What do you want?"

"It's not so much what I want but what *you* want. I'm here to make a deal."

"Deal?"

"Yes." The doctor's malevolent gaze fell on Francis's daughter. "I can spare her from death."

"You don't have that power. Not over life and death." Francis couldn't help a slight bit of hope that entered his voice. "Do you?"

"Over life?" The doctor made a dismissive wave with his hand. "No, not over life. But death?" A slight shrug and his gaze refocused on Francis. "When it comes to death, I have a little bit of pull."

"That's not possible," Francis croaked.

"Possible? You deign to tell me what is possible?" In a flash, the doctor's eyes were obsidian pools once more, and the fear returned to Francis's chest. "Look at me, Francis, and tell me what is possible."

"How?" Francis managed to ask around the lump in his throat.

And just like that, the doctor's eyes were normal brown eyes, and the sarcastic smile was back as he appeared to ponder the question.

As Francis watched the doctor, it occurred to him that the doctor had not moved from his original spot. He stood halfway between the bed and the door, immobile. The lack of movement was almost predatory, like the stillness of a lion in the midst of hunting a gazelle.

The doctor finally spoke.

"It started in the Garden when death entered the world. You're welcome for that, by the way. Before the Fall, it was only his game. Sitting on his throne, making all the calls, and hoarding all the glory. After the Fall, things got interesting." He chuckled to himself. "When death entered the world, I found I had some influence. Real influence. Power." He chuckled again, as if remembering some ancient cosmic joke. "In the beginning it was boring. You lived—" he held up one hand and raised the other, "—and yet didn't die. Boring!" His sinister cackle rang out.

Francis found himself frozen to his chair as he listened to the creature.

"So, I started to manipulate the shape of death," the doctor explained. "The curvature, or arc, if you will. Much like a doctor in a lab, I found I could create new forms of death in my own image. Death became fun. Fun to witness, fun to be a part of. Bubonic plague, Spanish flu, AIDS, cancer." He trembled in pleasure as he named each. "Only a sample of what I can do—of what I *did* do."

Francis spoke. "But you can't control who lives and who dies. Only God can."

This simple statement caused a brief flare of insane rage to flicker across the doctor's face.

"I can't control the who, the when, or the how, at least on the macro level ... but I can *affect* the how. I can and have shaped the how. Just look at the world! You think he introduced pain and suffering? No! That was me! Or should I say 'us'"—the sarcastic grin was back—"you and

I, Francis. Man and strife." He snickered at his play on words.

"Then how can you spare my daughter?" Francis asked. The persistent pitiful tone of hope leaked into his voice.

"I can slow or even stop the progression of the death currently eating her alive. The ravenous plague eating her brain is my creation, and as such, it bends to my will." He looked at Francis. "I can spare your daughter this death. I've done it before, and I can do it again."

"Then do it," Francis challenged. "Show me your power."

The doctor laughed. "No, Francis. It doesn't work like that. *I* don't work like that."

"Why do you keep saying 'I' as if you're the devil?" Francis asked. "I thought you weren't him? And if you're not, how do you have any power?" Francis didn't know where his courage to challenge this creature came from.

"Don't get caught up in the details, Francis." The doctor's tone grew ominous. "Think of me as the glove on the hand, the tongue in the mouth, the blade of the knife." His eyes darkened perceptively. "'I am who I am.'" He laughed, amused at his own blasphemy.

"What do you want?" Francis asked the question, already certain of what the answer would be.

"Ah," the doctor said eagerly, "now we come to the best part." He locked eyes with Francis. "For the recovery of your daughter, a small price. I only require your soul, Francis. Your timeless, immortal soul."

THE DEAL

Francis Neagley felt the air in his chest compress with the weight of the moment. He wasn't shocked by the price. He'd expected it. What weighed on him was the tangible desire to say yes. He wanted this. He wanted his daughter out of this God-forsaken hospital bed and at home where she belonged. A large part of him wanted to throw himself at this opportunity, no matter the cost. Another part in him, a small part, was horrified by the prospect of dealing with this creature. This force in him was no bigger than a seed, but it warred with his inner darkness, screaming at him.

No deal! Do not make this deal. Do NOT!

These two forces wrestled for control of Francis while he sat frozen in his chair, staring at the doctor. Like any good salesman, the doctor sensed the indecision in his prospective customer and immediately launched into his sales pitch.

"Why the reluctance, Francis?" he drawled seductively. "You want the cancer out of your daughter. I stand here offering you the opportunity to save her, and you pause?" The doctor folded the clipboard in his arms against his chest. "Just tell me. Put it in your own words, Francis."

"My soul?" Francis muttered while looking at the husk of his daughter. "My soul?"

"You're not using it, are you?" the doctor asked amusedly. "A moment ago, you were railing at him. Promising all kinds of things. Ridiculous things. And here I ask for something you're not even interested in, and you freeze? Why? At some misplaced loyalty? Is that it?"

The dark force in Francis rallied to this logic. Did he owe allegiance to anyone?

Yes! screamed the seed in response, but it was ignored. "My soul? But God ... he ..."

"*God?*" roared the doctor, but then regained his control. The cold, lethal softness of his speech seemed to echo with more volume than the previous word. "God? What has he done for you, Francis? Other than empty promises and a dead and dying family?"

Francis recoiled at the doctor's pure, icy hatred, and couldn't find his voice.

"I mean, look," the doctor said, as he gestured toward the frail body in the hospital bed. "Do I have to say anything else?"

"But it's your disease. You claimed it," Francis said weakly.

"Yes," the doctor agreed. "But I didn't decide it was her time. Even you admit I have no control over that."

Again, Francis had no answer.

"Listen to me," the doctor cajoled. "Don't cling to something you don't want for some noble reason you can't even define. Let go and say it."

Francis looked at his daughter while he spoke. "You're asking for something that has already been pledged. It's not mine to give."

"Isn't it?" asked the doctor.

"I promised ..."

"To what? Serve a God who's failed you at every turn? You don't even serve him any longer because you know. You know it's a lie. You led a church that, at the first sign of your weakness, cut you loose without batting an eyelash. And what was that weakness?" The doctor was relentless. "The death of your wife at the hands of a maniac."

"Don't!" Francis warned as he stood.

The doctor held up his hands in a placating gesture but continued. "Brenda, right?"

Francis collapsed back into the chair at the sound of that name. The anguish in his face conveyed the power of the moment.

"Brenda," the doctor's voice slithered, "was murdered, and you got lost in your grief. Your church tried to help with pies, casseroles, flowers, cards. Pitiful. Casseroles?" He spat the words. "You've got to be kidding me. And when they couldn't reach you through such flimsy means? They abandoned you, hired another pastor, and told you it was 'only until you get back on your feet.' But, of course, that was a lie. No one wanted to get close to you, as if they'd catch what you had. So, they played church and at the first opportunity jettisoned the dead weight." The creature pointed at Francis. "Meaning you."

"That's not how it happened." Francis tried to respond but found his unspoken feelings mirrored in what the doctor had just said. "They meant well, it's just—"

"What? *Meant well?* You sound pathetic," the doctor mocked. "You know I'm right. They used you. They used you for twenty years and then left you broken and hollow. I should know. I've heard some of your quietest words. When you thought you were alone, you voiced the truth."

Francis remembered all the times he'd yelled at his empty house. Cursing the people who'd betrayed him, berating the God who left him, and embracing the self-loathing he felt for doing it.

"Yes," the doctor encouraged. "You remember."

"I don't believe anymore," Francis whispered.

"You don't believe?" The doctor laughed softly. "Then why are we having this conversation? Who were you talking to when I interrupted if you don't believe?"

Francis again had no answer.

"Oh, you *believe*, all right." The confidence of the doctor was certain. "We know faith is not the problem. You know there's a God, like you know there's a devil. It's just where your faith lies that's at issue here."

Francis looked at him and felt the truth in those words. Faith was not the problem. He still believed in God. What was eating him alive was not faith that God was real, but lack of confidence that God cared. He saw the rubble of his life—the dead wife, the church that had abandoned him, his dying daughter. Questions haunted him—does God care? And if not, can I serve a God who doesn't?

He was no longer certain of those answers, and that uncertainty had led to this moment.

Where did his allegiance lie? With God? With his daughter? With this ... doctor?

The doctor, sensing the moment, slowly stalked toward the hospital bed. Francis saw his approach and stood protectively. The doctor smiled at his show of paternal care.

"Would a God," the doctor began in a musing tone, stopping at the foot of the bed not two feet from Francis, "would a God who cares for you let this happen? A church, a wife, a daughter, lost to the whims of—what? Fate? 'To work for the good of those who love God and are called according to his purpose?' Drivel! Rubbish! He's a tyrant, Francis!" His voice blazed. "Take, take, take. That's what he does. I don't want to take from you, I want to give. All I ask is for you to give me a piece of yourself. A piece the other doesn't deserve."

The doctor laid his hand on the bed and Francis found himself lunging across the two feet protectively. In a violent whirlwind, the doctor's hands were on Francis's throat as he lifted the man off the ground. The doctor's eyes were an evil abyss as Francis choked, dangling in the air.

"Don't, Francis," the doctor's voice grated. "I'm not to be trifled with. I don't care about you or your pathetic daughter." Francis was purpling from lack of oxygen. "At least I won't lie to you like he did. Promise you I love you while I take your family. Tell you it will be all right while I betray you in secret. I abhor you. But—"

And just like that, Francis found himself in his chair holding his daughter's hand and looking at the doctor as he stood where he originally was. The doctor's eyes were soft brown, and the smile was back.

"I will do as I say," the doctor promised congenially, as if he'd never held Francis suspended and strangling a moment before. "I will halt the death of your daughter. She will live until she dies, and your soul will be mine when you die. A fair deal with both parties knowing the truth."

The violence of the moment, the frankness of the deal, and the grief in his heart all worked to overcome Francis. Was it as simple as that? Were God and all his promises an elaborate fraud, a scam perpetrated by a callous overlord?

Had the majority of Francis's life been lived in service to a lie?

For some unknown reason he couldn't reconcile his heart's knowledge with these questions. Hearing his own past thoughts echoed back by this creature unveiled something he thought was lost. With that unveiling, a decision solidified in his chest.

The doctor, sensing something, tried to speak, but was interrupted by a small, quiet voice.

"Excuse me?"

Francis and the doctor turned to see a small child, a little girl, standing in the doorway. Her mother lingered behind her with an apologetic look on her face. The little girl looked at Francis expectantly.

Francis responded, "Yes, darling."

The little girl was clutching a stuffed animal in her hands. *She can't be more than seven*, Francis thought, as the child walked slowly into the room. She held out the animal, a stuffed bear.

"Can I give Pooh to you?"

"Me?"

"Yeah," the girl said meekly. "You look sad."

"I am," Francis confessed, and the girl stepped closer. Wordlessly she laid the bear in his lap.

"Thank you," Francis said.

The girl promptly turned and ran back to her mom. They left just as quietly as they had come.

Francis stared at the bear.

DECISION

"I've counseled so many families in my life." Francis squeezed the bear softly in his hands, watching it bend and reshape.

"That's because your God is a taker!" the doctor hissed from his place near the wall.

"So many families," Francis continued softly, his gaze fixing on his daughter, "and I never truly felt like I had given them less than the truth they needed. I told them about God's love, his purpose and plan, and explained how God would never leave them. The whole time I thought I was giving them some deep theological balm—some magical healing formula to make everything okay." He shook his head, ashamed. "I never knew the depth of their pain or the complete void where my words fell. I may as well have been trying to douse a forest fire, one thimble of water at a time."

"Yes," the doctor said eagerly. "So, you see?"

Francis continued, and as he did his face remained turned toward his daughter.

"When I lost Brenda ... no, when she was taken from us ... I was brutally baptized in grief. In an instant, I knew how inadequate any words of consolation were. As person after person told me how sorry they were and how they were praying for me, I learned the depth of my ignorance. I wanted a reason why Brenda was gone, not comfort for my loss. I wanted someone to come alongside me and rail at the heavens.

"The reason I was unreachable to my church afterwards was not because they couldn't reach me, but that I didn't want to let it go. When they replaced me, it was a relief. Yes, I was hurt that they'd cut me loose, but in a deeper place I was relieved. Relieved I wouldn't have to face them or their concerned looks again."

"This is how your God cares?" the doctor asked. "This is the reason you owe him loyalty?"

Francis didn't seem to hear. "It was Sarah who brought me out of that place. After weeks, maybe months of darkness, she was the one who led me back into the light."

Francis Neagley smiled warmly at his daughter.

"She didn't say a word. We would just sit there together watching TV or reading a book. She'd hug me or kiss my cheek at random times, letting her love coax me back to life. It worked too. Her acts of kindness and love … they saved me. She was a gift from God."

"Gift from God?" the doctor asked sarcastically. "More like the carpet to be pulled from under you. God was playing you like Lucy with her football. You're poor Charlie Brown!" He gestured toward the bed. "You're looking at your gift from God, dying in front of you."

"She never left the church," Francis said softly. "I thought I'd lost my faith. I'd watch her still attending services, coming home happy, and I started to wonder … I started to long for it. To believe again. And then we got the diagnosis."

"Yesss." The word sounded like steam from an old radiator. "The other shoe drops. The true face of God is revealed," the doctor said softly.

Francis stared at his daughter with wonder. His eyes drank her in, and he seemed to gain strength from her.

"I told you I didn't believe anymore."

"Your words," the doctor agreed, his tone hearty.

"Yes, my words," Francis continued. "But like you said, I still do. I believe in God. I just needed to be shown where my loyalty lies."

"And where is that?" The doctor leaned in expectantly.

"There is a place in the Bible where Jesus addresses the crowd and answers questions. He talks about a tower that fell, killing dozens of people. He asks if it was because of their sin that they were killed. Was there something in their past that killed them, or was there some unforeseen reason God would have to take them out? Jesus doesn't answer the question directly but challenges them for their lack of faith."

"So, he blames them!" the doctor said angrily.

"No," Francis countered. "No, he didn't. I had to read this over and over to get it. I wanted some direct reason as to *why* the tower fell and who was to blame. What did they do to deserve death? Why would God cause the tower to fall on them? I couldn't understand."

"Because there's nothing to understand! He's a tyrant!" the doctor interrupted.

Francis went on, undaunted. "I get it now. He wasn't ducking the question. He didn't leave the question unanswered. The answer is right there."

The doctor's eyes narrowed as Francis spoke.

"We see tragedy, and we want someone to blame. We want a *reason*. And when we can't find one, then we look to heaven in anger. Jesus didn't ask the question because there is a legitimate reason that would calm the grief within us. He asked because he wanted to expose the hypocrite within us. He knew no answer would be good enough for us. Think about it—is there any reason we would accept for the loss of a loved one? Anything God could tell us to make us understand the hole in our hearts? Jesus asked the question because he wanted us to come to the truth of the matter."

"Which is?" the doctor asked weakly, for he sensed Francis was crawling out of his grasp.

"That sometimes ..." Francis looked at the doctor, "sometimes towers fall. Sometimes tragedy hits us and there's no purpose behind it, no ultimate plan. The towers just fall. And we shouldn't go digging through the rubble, searching for some elusive reason to rebuild our lives. Sometimes there *is* no reason. We just have to believe that as we clear away the disaster, brick by painful brick, that God is still with us." Francis turned his gaze back upon his daughter.

"Like Sarah was there for me when we lost Brenda. Quietly sitting with me, holding me and loving me back to life. That's how it works. That's how he works."

"So, you'll lose your daughter," the doctor asked, his tone a sneer, "for this pathetic revelation? Because towers fall?"

"She's not gone yet." Francis gripped her hand as he leaned forward and slipped the stuffed bear under her arm. "And I'm going to try to do for her as she did for me."

With that he began to talk to his dying daughter. "I remember when you graduated high school, and …"

The doctor saw his opportunity evaporate, and he stalked from the room.

CHAPTER 3

LOVE APPROVED

How can love feel like betrayal? Loving someone shouldn't feel like this. Alex Epps sat at his desk, staring at his computer screen, thinking about his home life. He was supposed to be working on spreadsheets for an upcoming meeting, but his mind wouldn't focus on the numbers. How could he spend time on profits and margins when the rest of his life was in shambles? The answer—he couldn't.

That was why for the last three hours he'd been sitting at his desk and looking at his phone. He knew he should call his son, to tell him he loved him and would never stop loving him, but something in him saw that love as a betrayal of God. When he considered that idea, it seemed so absurd. Love as a betrayal of God? But in this case, it sure felt like betrayal.

He wasn't a pastor. He'd never been schooled in the theology of love and God. How could he, an accountant accustomed to crunching numbers, not Scriptures, reconcile the battle raging within him? Every Scripture he ran to seemed to point him toward his son, but when it came time for him to actually cross the divide, he floundered. Failed. Never had it been harder to love his son, or to express that love, than right now.

Brandon, his son, was sixteen, and that age alone was enough to pit father against son. Raging hormones, aggressive wit, high school drama, all the classic teenage battles. Add to that a father who was stubborn and aloof and a mother who was ever-present—the formula equaled a divided household. Alex tackled those issues in prayer every night and read his Bible for guidance. But every time he felt like he had a plan, when the time came to execute it, the situation would backfire. Emotions would boil over, feelings would be hurt, and all the combatants would flee to their rooms to lick their wounds. Nothing was ever truly accomplished.

The meeting with his pastor the week before had left him feeling more condemned than anything. Not that his pastor had made any negative comments. To the contrary. His pastor had urged him to step out in love and trust God to make a way. Never once did Alex feel anything except complete acceptance and love in that meeting, but for reasons he didn't know, he left the church feeling like a failure. Even having that meeting and admitting the struggle in his house only added to the great divide in his heart. He'd thought he'd done a good job raising his son and now ... now he couldn't even say "I love you" to Brandon. What an utter and total failure he was as a father.

"Forget this." Alex sighed and clicked the mouse on his computer, closing the accounting program. There was no reason to have it open when he wasn't paying attention. He reached into his desk drawer and grabbed his cigarettes and lighter, thinking maybe a smoke break would clear his mind. Smoking? Just another item on the list of Alex Epps's struggles, right behind being a good husband and failing as a father. He left his office in a hurry, not wanting to think about things any longer. It had been a long morning.

On his way out of the building, he swung by the lunchroom. The twisting hallways of his office building always somehow led a person by the employee cafeteria. The smells of Salisbury steak and gravy wafted out and caused his stomach to grumble, reminding him of his missed breakfast. The Salisbury steak smelled good.

Next thing he knew, he was behind Suzy from Marketing, in line for the lunchtime fare.

"Hey, Alex," Suzy greeted him politely.

"Hey to you too." Even though he didn't feel particularly chatty, he felt obligated to continue. "How's the family? Is Johnny out of the hospital?" Her two-year-old suffered from chronic asthma that had him in and out of the local medical center.

"He's fine," Suzy assured him, "but thanks for asking."

The line moved closer, and they picked up trays before being served. They were at the register before Suzy spoke again.

"Did you hear about Steve?" She nodded toward a woman sitting alone, finishing her lunch. "Or I guess it's Stacy now."

A pang of despair echoed in Alex's heart even though there was no judgment in his coworker's tone.

"He went through with the surgery, huh?" Alex's response was uncertain.

"Yeah, I guess so," Suzy said. "Well, good for him ... er, her." Alex made a noncommittal sound as they each paid for their meals and took a seat together. They ate in silence until Suzy spoke.

"How are Marge and the boys?"

Alex speared a piece of Salisbury steak. "Good ... well, not good, but we're trying to find our way."

"I saw Brandon's latest YouTube post," Lucy began awkwardly. "It was ... interesting. He does seem to be finding his way."

Alex shrugged and scowled. He and Lucy were cool, but he'd left his office to get away from the subject. Lucy read the look on his face and backpedaled.

"I'm sorry," she said honestly. "I can tell you don't want to talk about it."

"Thanks, Suz," Alex said with feeling, and went back to eating his lunch. After a few more bites he felt compelled to respond to Suzy's heartfelt words. "You know we're Christians, and ..."

Suzy looked confused. "What does that have to do with anything?"

"Well, I don't know," Alex continued defensively. "It's just that stuff like this is hard to deal with. It's hard to explain. Sorry, no offense meant, Suzy."

"None taken. I get it." Suzy looked over at the table where Stacy sat. A commotion was brewing involving two other male employees seated there. "What's going on over there?"

They both looked over to where laughter was flowing. Something in Alex knew it wasn't communal laughter but a weaponized form of joy. Stacy watched the two men, tensed as if she might slap their faces at any moment, and the men seemed to enjoy that.

For Alex, looking at Stacy was disorienting because when they'd met, she'd been Steve and had looked much different. All the masculinity was gone now, replaced by makeup and long curly hair. The medications he'd taken had changed his body and voice, only adding to the confusion of those who knew him. Steve had slowly changed into Stacy, and the transformation had left Alex unsure of how to interact. Now Alex felt protective as he watched the confrontation growing.

"Steve ... Stacy ... sir ... ma'am?" The man's words floated on the air, full of derision and antagonism. Laughter followed, and Alex found himself rising from his seat. He knew one of the antagonists, Tim, from church. The frustration of Alex's family life had found an outlet as he stalked over to the table where the three sat.

They saw him coming, and the smile on Tim's face stayed put, thinking he'd found another ally. Stacy looked ready to either bolt or attack but remained seated. The other man looked uncertain, made so by Alex's arrival.

Alex held Stacy's eye as he spoke. "What's up, Stacy?"

Stacy exhaled as she realized she wouldn't have to battle Alex too.

"Not a lot, Alex. How are you?" The high-pitched voice was new.

"I'm good." Alex looked to Tim and his friend. "What's up, Tim? Y'all all right?"

"We're fine," Tim responded warily as he sensed Alex might not be an ally after all. "Just talking with Steve here. Seeing how he's doing."

"You forget, Tim," the other hissed. "My name is Stacy."

"Is it?" Tim asked innocently. "You sorta looked like this dude I used to know named Steve." His friend laughed, and Alex felt a rising wave of disgust and self-condemnation.

"Tim," Alex said, trying and failing to keep his tone even, "why don't you lay off? Go sit somewhere else."

Tim scoffed. "Of course, you'd feel that way about him. Ain't that right, Steve?"

Stacy got up angrily and stormed out of the cafeteria. Alex watched her go with a broken heart. He looked back at Tim's sarcastic face and saw a mirror. The anger he'd felt dissipated, and he felt only sorrow. He sat down across from his brother in Christ and looked him in the eye as he spoke.

"Is this what it's come to?" he asked tiredly.

"What?" Tim asked belligerently. "I was just talking to a coworker."

"Yeah, yeah, I saw that. When the Bible said Jesus ate with tax collectors and sinners, I just didn't picture a meal like this."

Tim had the decency to look chagrined, but asked, "You judging me, Alex?"

Alex sighed sadly. "No, Tim. Just thinking out loud is all. I understand you more than you'd think, brother."

"Is that right?"

"Yes, unfortunately." Alex rose from the table. "Pray for me, brother, and I'll pray for you."

"What for?" Uncertainty filled Tim's voice. Of all the things he was expecting Alex to say, this wasn't it.

"That God softens our hearts so we can love like Christ does." And with that he turned and left the breakroom, heading for a much-needed cigarette.

Alex sat at the bus stop at the edge of his office building's lot. Employees weren't allowed to smoke on company property, so anyone wanting a quick refuge had to walk the hundred or so yards to the bus stop on the corner. Alex smoked his cigarette angrily, pulling on it like he was punishing his lungs for the encounter he'd just gone through. In a way, he was punishing himself. Tim's words had struck too close to home, both literally and figuratively, and seeing them wielded so brutally added more fuel to his fire of self-condemnation. He just wanted to love God and his family. Was that so much to ask?

He flicked his cigarette into the street half-finished and ran his hands through his hair in frustration. So distracted was he that he didn't realize he was not alone until the person next to him spoke.

"One of those days, huh?"

Alex looked to his left to find Steve—no, Stacy, he reminded himself—sitting next to him, removing a cigarette from a pack and lighting up.

"Yeah," Alex agreed. "One of those days."

They sat in awkward silence for a few seconds before Stacy spoke again.

"Thanks for running interference back there."

"Sure." Alex exhaled forcefully, shaking his head.

Stacy looked at him steadily until Alex looked over and met the look. Stacy seemed to come to a decision, and asked quietly, "What did Tim mean back there?"

"I don't know what you're talking about." Alex looked away.

"He said, 'Of course, you'd feel that way.' What did he mean by that?"

She's not going to let it go. Alex clenched his jaw while he fought inside himself. He didn't want to have this conversation again, especially not with an unbeliever, but sometimes a wound speaks without the wounded's consent. He sighed and started talking.

"Tim goes to my church."

"That guy goes to church?" Stacy looked incredulous.

"Yeah, he goes to my church, and some things my family's dealing with have come to light." A few seconds passed. "My son Brandon, whom I love with my whole soul, came out last month in the teens' youth group. Not only that, but he believes he's ... uh ... a woman trapped in a man's body." The words seemed to choke their way out.

Stacy sensed his conflict. "So, Brandon is transgender?"

"Well, yes, I suppose so."

"Congratulations."

Alex looked at Stacy, not knowing if she was making a joke or being serious. "I don't think congratulations are in order, Stacy."

"Why not?" Stacy asked, then pulled on her cigarette. "Your son's done a brave thing. It's not easy to fight that battle."

Alex shut down his immediate response and tried to clear his tone of any judgment that might bleed through.

"I know you feel that way, but in my family's belief system it is wrong for ... well, for a man to become a woman." This wasn't coming out right. "It doesn't jibe with the Bible. No offense, Stacy."

"None taken," his coworker responded. "You said your family's belief system?"

"Yeah."

"Apparently not your whole family," Stacy said with a smirk. "I'm sorry, I don't mean to be glib."

"Yes, you do."

Stacy chuckled. "Yeah, I guess I do. I just don't know why you Christians are so uptight. Always worried about the wrong things. Never about the right things."

"To us," Alex began seriously, "this is the right thing. God created us as man and woman. To alter that is wrong because we would be playing God."

"How so?"

The look of pure curiosity on Stacy's face froze Alex with its honesty.

"Well, if God put you in that body, a male body, and you believe it's the wrong body, then essentially God made a mistake. God doesn't make mistakes. If you felt that way, then you should have borne that cross and asked God to help shoulder the burden and set you free from that struggle. What you did was ... well, wrong, according to the Bible."

"Which is always right?" Stacy said deadpan.

"Yes," Alex said confidently. "And on top of that you are, in the Biblical and genetic sense, still a male having sex with males. And homosexuality is also sinful."

"Sinful?" Stacy spat. "Kind of like your friend Tim's behavior."

Alex was ashamed. "Yes, like that."

They sat in silence again, gathering their thoughts. Stacy spoke first.

"I feel like I shouldn't like you because of what you just said."

Alex sighed, disappointed. "I know. My son feels the same way."

"But I saw what you did back there in the breakroom. I can see what it's costing you. Why can't you do that for your son? For Brandon?"

"I don't know."

"You don't know?" Stacy laughed.

Alex felt his anger rising. "No, I don't."

"See? This is what I was talking about." Stacy looked at him with pity. "Always worried about the wrong things. You came to my defense in front of an entire cafeteria and we're barely friends. You call me Stacy when everyone else still struggles, and you never avoid me. Yet you can't do the same for your son?"

This was the crux of his battle. Alex struggled for words. "It's different with you."

"How so?" Stacy reiterated gently.

"You're not my son. You're a—barely a friend, and not a Christian. It's easier for me to accept you because ... well, because I'm not trying to guide you down the right path like I am my son. You're a grown person and free to live your life ... but Brandon? I feel like if I accept his decision, it would be ... a passive approval of his choice. And that approval feels like a betrayal of my faith. How can I accept my son, yet not approve of his lifestyle?"

"I don't know," Stacy said honestly. "And I suppose Brandon sees your non-approval as a form of betrayal himself?"

"Exactly!" Alex agreed. "I love my son with my whole soul. I would die for him, but I can't approve of his choice. Accept it? Yes. But never approve. Why do acceptance and approval have to be linked?"

"I guess that's how we humans are wired."

Alex and Stacy once again lapsed into silence, each lost in their own thoughts. For Alex, this conversation was only a rehashing of numerous other conversations he'd already had with his pastor and wife, neither of which had been able to bring these two things into agreement. Acceptance and approval. He wanted one without the other, and his son demanded them both.

"I think the answer is love." Stacy spoke into the void.

Alex looked over with genuine need. "Love?"

"I think that love can bridge the gap. Your son seems to want your approval, but I think he really just wants your love."

"I do love him," Alex said desperately.

"Yes, but it's a stipulated love, and that kind of love feels false. You have to love him with action too, not just words ... like you did for me earlier. You have to see him in his fabulous state." Stacy stopped and preened. "And not flinch. If you flinch, you'll lose him."

"I feel like I already have."

"Maybe ... maybe not."

"How do I not flinch?"

"Honey, that's between you and Brandon." Stacy stood to leave, but before departing turned with a last question and a wink.

"What would Jesus do?"

Alex watched his friend leave, thinking, what *would* Jesus do? The well-used cliché held a deep wisdom as such clichés often do. He was sure that in the days Jesus spent with "tax collectors and sinners," there had to be some gay people in the crowd. Did Jesus stop the festivities to ask them to leave? Did he explain to them that although he accepted them in all their brokenness, he did not approve of their life choices? For some reason that didn't seem likely. There would've been a lot of breaks in the meal as Jesus explained to each faction of sinners the difference between acceptance and approval. The more Alex thought about it, the more he came to believe that love was the answer. Love in action, not in word. Love in a shared piece of bread, an open conversation, an unflinching look, a shared community, and ultimately love on a cross.

Unwavering, immovable, unashamed love.

What would Jesus do? Alex laughed to himself. Love, that's what he'd do. His decision made, Alex gathered himself and headed to his car. Today would be a half day at work. He needed to go to have a conversation with his son.

CHAPTER 4

INHERITANCE

FISSURE

"I want to tell you what happened."

"It's okay ..."

"No, I need to tell you ..."

"I'm here, my love."

Deep breath.

"I was thirteen ..."

The noonday sun blazed high at its zenith as I dug through the dusty earth. With no wind to speak of, my hair was a sticky mess pasted to my forehead, and I was constantly trying to brush the long blonde hair out of my face with dirty hands. That only served to put a ring of grime along my hairline. My tank top and jeans were past filthy, but what did I care? I'd left the Barbies behind when I was six, and now at thirteen I was consumed only with reading and with all things archeological. Most girls stayed up all night talking about boys with their friends or had sleepovers where they'd spend all night gossiping. Not me.

I read at a college level, was three grades ahead in school, and was obsessed with carbon dating, not boy dating. I'd left most of my childhood friends behind long ago. In the high society where I was raised, I was an aberration, an oddity. Little girls didn't play in the dirt. But I did, and I didn't care, which thinned my social calendar dramatically. I was thirteen going on thirty, and I enjoyed the solitude of my higher thinking.

My parents doted on me and my siblings. My brother, Roger, was the oldest by five years, and my sister, Pamela, was two years younger than Roger. Even with the age differences, by the age of five I had already caught up to my sister in intelligence, and by nine I was helping Roger with his high school algebra. Roger couldn't have been more proud of that. He loved me fiercely and always showed off his "genius little sis" to his friends, having me do random math problems in my head. For some reason, though, my intelligence pushed my sister away from me. It may have been the attention I received or the fact I acted older than my years and she younger than hers. Which sort of made me the older sister by default, not by design. I loved Pamela and always yearned for a relationship with her, but there was always friction between us.

My parents, as I said, doted on us. My mom was a stay-at-home wife, and even though we had the means to hire a nanny, she eschewed any suggestion to hire one. She was a constant, loving presence in our lives, and she always encouraged us in our passions.

My father ... my father was complicated. He loved us with his whole heart but was raised in a time where stoicism was prized above emotion. He was a pillar of strength but could make you feel like a rock star with barely a smirk, and his raised eyebrow was a sign of approval. We kids lived for those infrequent small moments of acceptance and love he doled out. Not to say he didn't love us or was cold—he was just reserved and showed his love mostly by the way he provided for us and by his constant presence in our lives.

My father was a high-powered attorney from a line of highly successful lawyers dating back generations. Which is where, I believe, our differences found their root. Women of his era acted a certain way and fit into a certain box of propriety and dignity. They didn't have to be wives or figureheads, nothing that archaic, but they certainly didn't act like boys, which is how my father viewed my later development.

When it was obvious that I was special, my father wanted me to focus my intellect toward the courtroom or the surgical field, something respectable and profitable. But at ten years old, I wouldn't be steered toward something so boring when there was actual history waiting to be unearthed in the backyard!

The more he pushed, the more I grew resolved, and the larger the space between us grew. As the stacks of *National Geographics* and *Archaeological Digest* grew on my dresser, the less time my father and I spent together. As a child with a young adult mind, I struggled to validate my passion, and when it was rejected, I took that personally. It didn't help that my father and I were more alike than either of us would have admitted. We both were stubborn and blessed with an inner resolve of self-righteousness. Admitting defeat was not in our genetic makeup.

Which was why, at thirteen, I found myself kneeling in the dirt a half mile from our house. It was my father's birthday, and I was searching for the perfect gift. Instead of getting him the requisite tie or aftershave, I'd decided to get him something from my heart. The week prior, I'd discovered an area of our property that hid a treasure of buried Native American artifacts. Later I'd learn that my mother had gathered artifacts purchased at a museum years before, buried them, and then suggested that I try digging in that area, but that's a story for another time. What's important is that at that moment my little trowel and brush were uncovering a perfectly preserved arrowhead. A perfect specimen! As I gently unearthed my gift, I knew that my father would love it, and finally, he would accept my hobby as something more. This would be the day we'd forget about our past bouts, and I'd find acceptance again in his eyes.

As the arrowhead came free of the dirt, I picked up the jewelry box lined in cotton that I'd brought along. I placed the arrowhead inside and got to my feet with a huge smile of satisfaction. I was sweaty, dirty, tired, and absolutely filled with joy and pride. This would be a great day. Then I looked at my watch and realized I was late. I'd lost an hour somewhere in all that digging, and my father's party was already beginning.

I ran the entire way home, which didn't help my appearance any but only exacerbated an already sticky situation. When I got home the party was already in full swing, with the house full of family and friends sharing food and drink. Just as they announced it was time to open gifts, I hurried to the bathroom and took stock of just how filthy I was. I quickly washed my face and hands and toweled dry, but it helped nothing. I pulled my sweaty hair into a ponytail, which only highlighted the dirt in it, and sighed. I hurried outside to where my father was opening gifts from his family.

I pushed my way through the crowd of people with apologies until I was at the front of the group. Father sat on a patio chair with my mother beaming at him while he opened her gift.

Inside was a picture in a silver frame.

"What is this?" My father's voice was like an avalanche.

"That's us at our high school prom," Mother responded, "so you'll always remember where all this started."

"Thanks." Rare emotion choked his voice. "I love it."

They hugged, and our family broke into quiet applause. My mother caught my eye in that moment and smiled at me. She never noticed, or at least never acknowledged, my generally filthy state. I could come home covered in dirt and she'd scoop me up in a hug while wearing her

Sunday best. This time was no different. When they broke their embrace, my mother beckoned me forward.

Suddenly, my confidence left as I shuffled my way to them. All my adult pretentions fell away under my father's gaze. I could tell my disheveled state displeased him, which chiseled away another level of confidence. By the time I stood before them, I was five years old again. I held my gift forward, unwrapped, and to my horror, covered in grime.

"Happy birthday, Daddy!"

My mom sensed my discomfort and laid a hand on my father's shoulder as he accepted my gift. My father smiled tightly, caught between reproof for my appearance and genuine warmth of the moment.

"Thanks, honey," he said neutrally as he opened the box. It seemed as if the world stood still. My heart thudded in my chest, fresh sweat blossomed, and my breath caught in my lungs as I awaited his response. If there were any mumblings from the crowd, I couldn't hear them. I was in a bubble of silence.

The skin around my father's eyes crinkled, a grimace appeared on his face, and the verdict was in—*rejection*. He spoke, and even though his tone was polite and the words gentle, they didn't reach me.

"Oh, how nice. Thank you."

I was already pushing through the crowd to escape. I heard my mother's rebuke, but it only served to add to my shame. "Philip!"

"What?" he asked tightly.

"Annie, wait!" my mother called after me.

I made it into the house and dashed up to my room, slammed the door, and threw the lock. I jumped on my bed and wept into my pillow as my mom knocked gently on the door. I ignored her, lost in my world of grief and rejection. Eventually, sleep overcame me.

I awoke hours later to my parents fighting. Their voices crashed through the house in a battle waking me from my sleep. My parents never fought like this. Sure, they had fights, but screaming at each other? Never. I got out of bed and crept out of my room quietly, drawn to the combat. Somehow, I knew it revolved around me. As I crept down the hall, my sister poked her head out of her room and sneered at me.

"Look what you've done now!" she hissed, and then eased her door shut.

As I approached my parents' room, the voices became clear, and I peeked around the corner to watch the battle.

"I won't keep encouraging this nonsense," my father growled. "She needs to grow up! Digging in the dirt, wasting her talent."

My mother stood toe-to-toe with him, which wasn't easy for her physically. Father was huge, and she was a tiny woman, but she made up for it in passion. My father cringed when she poked his chest.

"That gift was from her heart. And *you*! You dismissed it!" My mother's tone was indignant, and Father cringed again. "Your daughter grew up years ago, and she found her talent in that dirt, but you refuse to see that. That gift is a piece of her, and by denying it, you deny her!"

"Better she gets the hard truth now than after she's wasted her chance at life." Father picked up my gift and tossed it in the trash can. "Our family doesn't scratch in the earth for pointless trinkets! We're Barringtons, for God's sake. Let that gift stay in the trash where it belongs."

"How dare you?" my mother gasped in disbelief.

I must've made some noise because at that moment my father made eye contact with me, and the small crack between us became a yawning fissure. A brief look of dismay crossed his face, but I wasn't sticking around for the next hammer blow to fall. I fled, and the course of my life was set.

Silence falls in the car as I finish my confession. My husband Freddy had held my hand as I unburdened my life's biggest regret, and now he lets the emotion of the moment settle. I can tell from the tears shining in his eyes he wants to cry on my behalf, but he holds back. That's why I love him so much. He's always thinking of me and choosing the perfect way to love me in each moment.

We sit in our rental car outside the lawyer's office that summoned us a week ago. The rest of the family is already inside, presumably waiting for us. I just can't build up the courage to go inside. I've always been brave, always able to find the strength to conquer over any obstacle, but my father's death has altered something inside me. Maybe it was my father's life and the enmity between us that powered me before and gave me that intangible resolve.

Since his death last week, I haven't been able to find my feet. Every waking moment has been surreal. I thought we'd have more time—time to heal the wound between us, time to say how sorry we were and how stupid we had both been over the last seventeen years. Now that opportunity is lost.

I've never told Freddy about that day. Never spoken of it to anyone. My husband always knew that something tragic had occurred between my father and me, but he never pushed too hard for the details. He sits there considering with a clinical eye the wound I've uncovered. He's a psychologist by trade, and I know he's gently sifting through the minutiae of my revelation. His mind is as quick as his heart as he reveals just how well he knows me.

"So, you're realizing now how much your father loved you." He speaks gently. "Even if he was a jerk that day."

I bristle at that, but then I see the smirk on his face that tells me he is only lightening the mood. I return the half smile.

"Yes. He failed me that day, and I held it against him for seventeen years. Seventeen years! And now he's gone."

"It's not your—"

"I know!" I cut him off, agreeing then contradicting. "But it was. I didn't ask for the rejection, and he deserved some of my anger, but seventeen years? You know how many times he's called me in the last decade? You've been there. I never gave him the chance to apologize. I always thought there'd be more time. I spent my life building accomplishments to prove him wrong, and now he's gone, and he's left me with only empty achievements."

"Honey," Fred reproves me, "your achievements are not empty. You have two doctorates and a respected position on the national archeological board. You've been published more times at thirty than most people in their entire lives, and you are married to the best man on earth. You're not empty."

I smile at him and love him even more. "I know in my head you're right, but not here." I touch my chest. "The two won't agree, and I can't grieve. Fred, I haven't even cried for my father. Not one tear!"

I can feel the unshed tears straining against my soul, begging for release that just won't come. I lower my head into my hands as a wave of sorrow and shame wash over me. Freddy gives me space for a heartbeat and then reaches over to me and draws me into his loving embrace. He murmurs softly in my ear, "It's okay, baby. It's okay."

I groan into his chest. It's all my grief will allow. My arms wrap around his back, and I pull into him as his voice rumbles in my ear.

"Let's pray before we go inside, okay?"

I nod in agreement, still wrapped up tight against his chest.

"Dear Lord, we need your strength and peace in this moment. Reach down and comfort our broken hearts and give us the courage to face down our giants. Touch my wife with your mercy. Let it cover her shame and relieve her guilt. Let us bring to you those burdens that aren't ours and lay them down at your feet. In Jesus's name ..."

The atmosphere in the lawyer's office is somber as we enter the conference room. My mother gets up from the large mahogany table and comes around to hug me.

"Annie." She has always called me by that name even though I've been insisting on Anne for years. It feels good. Obstinate motherly love.

"Mom." We hug tightly, and then, she returns to her seat.

Around the table are the various parties mentioned in my father's will. A representative from his lawyer's office occupies one seat. My sister and her husband Terry sit together. Terry nods with a small congenial smile. He has always been a nice man, unlike my sister who sits glowering at me. How such a beautiful woman can look so embittered is beyond me.

I breathe deeply as I wave in their direction, hoping to dispel some of the brewing animosity. It doesn't work. My sister scowls even deeper. The only open chairs are next to my brother Roger and his wife. He rises from his chair as we approach and wraps me in a warm hug.

"Annie." I can feel him trembling as he tries to hold it together. "I've missed you."

I return his embrace. "You too, big brother."

He and Freddy shake hands after we break the hug, and then, we all sit. The young lawyer sits at the end of the table with my father's last will and testament in her hands. She is a mousy, no-nonsense type of person who still somehow exudes comfort at this moment. She wears tortoiseshell glasses, and her eyes lock on each of us as she speaks.

"Thank you all for being here," she begins, "and let me express my heartfelt condolences to your family. Philip Barrington was a pillar in this community, as well as my mentor, and the world is less without him. I never thought we'd be sitting around this table so soon, but we are, and we'll handle it with the dignity and aplomb Philip would've expected of us." She pauses to allow us to silently agree with this instruction before continuing.

"The will is very succinct and concise, so we will get through this quickly together. Please do not interrupt the reading. If you have any concerns or are disgruntled in any way ... that's why we have probate court. You can address your issues there. Now that we have the instructions out of the way we can continue with Philip's wishes."

The room quiets as the lawyer opens the envelope containing the will and lays it on the table. Every person in the room will be affected by what comes next. The atmosphere in the room is not one of anticipated wealth, although great wealth is expected. It is communal anxiety because no one really wants to be in the room. Everyone would trade every penny of their inheritance to have the man who was lost back.

The lawyer turns the first page. "I will skip the legalese and jump to declarations of Philip's will." She begins to read.

Hello, family. I'm sorry we are all here, but I'm glad everyone is together again. You understand I am not an emotional man, so I will skip that part, knowing that all of you know that I loved you deeply.

To my fellow colleagues at Barrington, Brighton and Worth, I leave in your trust the sum of ten million dollars to be used to continue managing our pro-bono division at the firm. Use the money well and bless those less fortunate.

The lawyer from his firm nods gravely at this charge.

To my beautiful and amazing wife, Kristen, I knew you'd disapprove greatly if I left too much to you instead of to our children, so I won't. Instead, I leave all our properties and the amount of twelve million dollars to administer the upkeep. I loved you, my queen, more than the dawn loves the sun. I was blessed by your grace.

I look to my mother to see her radiant smile and tears streaming down her face.

To my doppelganger, my son, Roger. I was so proud to be your father. No son has ever been so steadfast. You're everything I wanted in a son. I leave you the amount of fifty million dollars to use in any way you deem fit. Let the fruit of my work bless your family.

My brother lowers his head onto the table and silently sobs. His wife gently rubs his back while whispering in his ear.

Pamela, stop scowling.

My sister looks surprised at my father's words spoken from the grave, then scowls deeper.

I love you, my strong, passionate, impertinent daughter. It warms my heart to know you are there with that look on your face, even now, and being the defender of the luckiest father to have ever lived.

My sister's face softens, then seeming to realize the façade has slipped, she scrunches up her face in challenge.

To you, my champion, I leave you the same amount of fifty million dollars to use however you deem appropriate. I'll love you always.

Pamela sits up straighter, accepting his charge.

And lastly, my daughter, Anne. I will keep words at a minimum, for I leave you with a letter explaining things. No daughter was ever more what a father didn't want, but in being so became more than I ever dared expect. Please accept this letter and box in lieu of monetary inheritance, for I pray the former is what you want rather than the latter, which I fear would just keep us apart.

I sit stunned. Everyone around the table looks shocked except for my mother, who has always truly known me.

I love you all. Never forget that.

It's been a few hours since the reading. I'm at home in my backyard swinging listlessly on a bench swing in our backyard. My husband is in the house. I can feel his eyes on me as he respects my wish to be alone, but still, he watches me with concern. He's worried about me. I understand. I haven't spoken since the reading, and I still clutch the letter and small box I silently accepted from the attorney. I'm building up the courage to open either of them, but I don't know which should be first.

The box? No. Why accept a gift without the sentiment attached? The letter first, then. Yes, the letter first. And why am I debating this so stoically? Shouldn't I be raving right now? My siblings get fifty million each, and I get a letter and a box? Yet I know intuitively that what's contained in these two items is going to change my world, and I think that's why I can't open them. Am I ready to move on? Do I want to? This has been the wall in front of me for seventeen years, my self-declared and self-imposed righteous belief that I was wronged. What was so clear and tangible before has now became petty and illusory.

My hands move of their own accord and begin opening the letter. I'd love to blame my hands for their betrayal, but as the letter opens revealing my father's flowing script, I am thankful for their duplicity. I sit staring at the page, and like a woman dying of thirst, I drink in his words as I begin to read.

Annie, my Annie, I pray that this letter brings you peace. I've spent so many years rehearsing what I would say to you, or how I would say it to you, if I had the chance. This is the fifth iteration of this letter, as I write it every year or so. Every time I write, I hope it is the last and we'll forgive each other, and this letter will become moot. I've tried calling you but never could reach you. Please. honey, don't blame yourself for that. I understand, and if anyone deserves the blame let it be with me. I failed you as a father, and it is my life's biggest regret.

That day years ago haunts me. As I've watched you grow into such a magnificent woman, the pride in my heart has overwhelmed me. I recognize now how tragic it was for me to dismiss your dream, a dream you are living now and thriving in. I've read every article ever published by you. I was at every graduation, and I silently thanked God when you found Fred. I know now those silent thanks should have been aloud. I should've fought for you. I shouldn't have accepted "no" from you. I should've humbled myself and been the father you deserved.

I love you, Annie Constance Barrington. I've always loved you. I NEVER stopped. I'm so sorry for that day. When I saw the brokenness in your eyes, I was filled with shame and allowed that shame to blind us. It should not have become shame for both of us. Please, my heart, lay it down. If you can, find a place in your heart to forgive your dad and go on to live a life full of the joy and peace you so richly deserve. Know that I am in Heaven looking down on you with a burning pride and a fierce love.

Enclosed in the box is a token that I've carried with me for years. I kept it on me the first time we battled this cancer, and I believe it pulled me through. This time God had different plans, so I want you to have it back. I love you so very much, Annie.

Love,
Dad

I sit trembling as I finish the letter. The emotional dam that has been holding me together seems to be straining at its foundation. All the unrequited feelings I've been withholding from life for almost two decades have been echoed in this letter. A sense of divine peace envelopes me as I realize that my father loved me just as much as I always loved him, maybe more so.

And that realization has freed something inside me. I want to be free again ... and suddenly, I am.

No more shame, no more guilt. no more anger. I simply let them go. And with that release, I find another well of love inside of me that I held for my father. A source that I haven't drawn from in years that is welling with strength. I draw from it now as I set the letter down and pick up the box beside me.

It's a small box, a jewelry box, and with bated breath, I ease open the lid. What lies inside causes the straining dam of emotion within me to burst, and unrestrained tears flow from my eyes as sobs rack my body. These are not tears of sadness, shame, or guilt. Instead, tears of joy, peace, and fulfillment.

Suddenly, Fred is there next to me, and he wraps me in his arms as the box falls to the ground. My inheritance stays gripped in my hand as I cling to my husband sobbing unashamedly. I push gently, and he breaks the hug slowly. I'm still crying with no words to say as I hold my hand out.

"What is it?" my husband asks with concern.

I hiccup and giggle at that absurdity, causing him to smile. We both watch my hand unfold revealing my inheritance hidden in its grip.

And there it sits, an arrowhead buffed to a dull shine.

CHAPTER 5

THIS IS IT

SO. THIS IS IT.

This is what it feels like to die. My legs can barely hold my weight, and my heart is in my throat. Literally. I thought that was something people always just said, like when they're exaggerating, because how can it actually feel like my heart is in my throat? It doesn't make sense, but it's true. I don't want to die! I'm only twelve, and my whole life is in front of me. Maybe I can escape. When they lead the next condemned one up onto the platform, I could use it as a distraction and try to slip away.

A dry cough rasps behind me, and I turn around to see my overseer staring right at me. His inscrutable gaze locks eyes with mine, and my bowels turn to water as he approaches. It's like he can smell my fear. He probably can, the monster. His clothes reek of cigarette smoke and his teeth are yellowed stumps as he leans down to speak to me.

"Don't worry." His voice tries to be soothing, but it comes out diabolical instead. "It'll be over before you know it."

That was supposed to be comforting? If my hands weren't locked in fear, I'd have scratched his eyes out. All I want to do is go home. I don't want to walk up onto that wooden walkway of death where I'll perish for the pleasure of some insane crowd. Everyone out there is a freak in my book. Weirdos that find satisfaction in the pain and fear of children.

The crowd roars its appreciation as the last condemned finishes their death throes and the next sacrifice is led on stage. The line gets shorter, and I shuffle forward a few steps. There is only one more person ahead of me. One more. Maybe I could slip backward in line to buy some time and hope that my parents can come to my rescue. They love me, right? Of course they do. They wouldn't let their only son suffer at the hands of a mob. Would they? Of course not. All I have to do is slip back a few spots and give them time to find me and get me out of here.

I try to act normal as I look behind me into the line of frightened faces. The girl behind me looks more scared than I feel, as if she may fall over and die this very second. The boy behind her is … smiling. He seems to be enjoying himself. The psycho! Don't you know you're about to die? Can't you hear the cheers as victim after victim is led to his or her death? I want to punch his stupid face. Wait! If he is so happy then he wouldn't mind switching places with me! All I must do is get his attention and—

"Ah!" That little girl just tried to bite me! She's still snarling at me like some dog.

"Don't even think about it," she warns. "You're next, not me!"

Well, so much for that idea. Looks like I'm next as the crowd roars again, and the next child is led up. But I'm only twelve. I haven't even kissed a girl, and I'm going to die before I get the chance! Well, there was that time last summer when Autumn Ray pecked me on the cheek, but I don't count that because it was on a dare, and I didn't even know it was coming until it was over. Why am I even thinking about this? I'm about to die, and I'm thinking about kissing a girl?

This is crazy. Okay, think, Javon, think! I could just start crying and maybe they'd have mercy on me. No, that's dumb. I'd just end up dying like some coward in front of hundreds of people. And what if Dad's out there? I can't let him down. I remember the talk we had last night as he tried to prepare me for this moment.

"You're strong, Javon," he'd said. I could tell he was feeling the fear too, because his grip on my shoulders was extra tight. "You can do this. When you get up there, just find me and your mother's face and focus on us until it's over. We'll be with you every step, Son."

Wait! That means he's not trying to get me out of this. He's out there right now with my mom, and they're going to watch. They're monsters too!

So there really is no way out of this. These are the last minutes on earth I'll spend, and I'm wasting them being terrified. I should be like ... defiant or something. Like in the movies. The stars don't feel fear and wait for their mommies and daddies to save them. They practically put the noose on their own necks and then they scream something cool like, "Freeeee-dommm!" before they die.

I should try to think of something like that to shout. Something totally heroic and brave that people will talk about after it's over, like "Did you hear Javon scream out when it was his turn?" "Yeah, then he died, but it was so brave!" Okay, so what do I scream out that will shame these animals?

Ooh. "Never agaaaaain!" That sounds pretty heroic. I'll need to look out into the crowd like I'm not afraid and make sure I don't pass out. That would totally wreck it. "Never agaaaaain!" and then *plop!* I pass out. That'd be even more embarrassing than not saying anything. All right, so defiance and heroism while I die, like a movie star.

"Javon Samuels, you're up. Let's go." The headsman ushers me forward.

Wait! What was I doing again? Oh my gosh, I forgot and now it's my turn! My legs aren't working. The headsman comes down the stairs to make me move.

"Come on, Javon," she commands, as my legs begin to work again. I follow her up the few stairs and onto the platform. With every step up, I know I'm closer to death. I don't want to move, don't want to help them kill me, but I'm led along like a sheep.

As we come up onto the platform and out from behind the curtains the crowd gets quiet. All I can hear is my own breathing and heartbeat. In front of me is some administrative ghoul holding a weird scroll and leering at me hungrily. I can tell this crazy person enjoys his job. I remember my dad's words at the last second and try to find my parents in the crowd.

I search the sea of faces looking for my beloved family. There! I see them looking at me and I try to take strength from them. My father's eyes are filled with tears as he watches me cross the stage. My mother mouths a final "I love you" toward me, but I can't find the strength to return it. I'm going to die, and I can't even tell her I love her. Well, I'll be brave then. I try to straighten my back and paint a weak smile on my face. Dad's not buying it, but I can tell he's proud of the effort. A tear trails down my mom's face as she holds her camera up. Wait, a camera? They're recording this! Monsters! Betrayers!

I close the gap on the platform finally and stand before the Administrator of Evil. He begins speaking, and I can't hear a word he's saying. It's drowned out by the pounding of my heart. He has me face the crowd as he makes his proclamations and I have to look into the faces of all the maniacs here to watch my demise.

Animals! You 're all animals! The thoughts steam through my mind in these last seconds. *One day this could be you! We'll see how you like it then,* I shout at them telepathically.

As the man beside me drones on, I can tell it's coming to an end. I finally focus in on what he's saying, and my mind finds peace, knowing it's finally over.

"And, ladies and gentlemen, Javon Samuels won the 2021 Young Writers of Renown Award this year. He has a bright future ahead of him! Let's hear it for this new graduate of Master's Elementary!"

The crowd erupts in applause, and I snatch my diploma from the principal's claws as I stagger off the stage. I'm so glad that's over. On to Junior High! I look back over my shoulder as I'm led off to see the terrified girl making her fearful way across stage.

Poor sucker.

CHAPTER 6

THE IRONY OF THE FOXHOLE (ADAPTED FROM THE PLAY)

"There are no atheists in foxholes."—*attributed to WWII Military Chaplain Thomas Cummings*

Moreover, brethren, I declare to you the gospel which I preached to you, which also you received and in which you stand, by which you are also saved, if you can hold fast that word which I preached to you— unless you believed in vain. 1 Corinthians 15:1-2 NKJV

FRONT LINE

"Dear Lord, I thank you for this beautiful morning. What a day it is to bask in your glory. You truly are magnificent, and I could not ask to have led a more blessed life."

Truer words were never spoken as Pastor Tristen Jordan prayed to his God. Sitting in the parking lot of the local Denny's in his 2015 Dodge Caravan, Tristen took stock of his charmed life. His two beautiful children, Bobby and Vanessa, were the light of his life, and he was married to his best friend.

Linda Jordan was the best partner he could ask for, and together they'd done great things for the Lord. They co-pastored a thriving church, ran an overseas ministry, and led couples' therapy twice a month. Most people called them a Power Couple. They just gave thanks to God. Tristen's parents and in-laws were still alive, major contributors to the family's strength. They brought a depth of wisdom that only eight decades of life could bring, and Tristen thanked God regularly for them. If there was a place in his life that was deficient, Tristen was unaware of its existence.

Life was good.

"Father, prepare my heart this morning. Let my words be your words. Let my love be your love. I am grateful for my friend, Jake, and I would ask your blessing on him. Even though he is at odds with you in his intellect, Lord, I ask that you draw near to his heart. Let the one teach the other. He's a good man, Father. Save him. In Jesus's name, amen."

Tristen finished the prayer and opened his eyes. Morning sunlight filled the van, and soft praise music played over the speakers. Could this be the day? The day that sixteen years of friendship was leading him to? Tristen prayed it was so. For sixteen years, he'd had the privilege of knowing his high school buddy, Jake Evans. They'd met at Ralston High School during their junior year and couldn't have made an odder pair. Tristen, football star and captain of the track team, was part of the high school elite, and Jake was the loner whose hyperintelligence kept him apart from the rest of his peers.

They met in US History class when the teacher had opened a debate on the pros and cons of the military industrial complex. Tristen had argued the pros, and Jake had argued the cons, with neither proving a decisive victory. The verbal sparring had led to a mutual respect and then their unlikely friendship. When a few years later Tristen gave his life to God, Jake took it upon himself to "save" his friend from intellectual suicide. As an ardent atheist, Jake found all faith absurd, Christianity especially so. He believed morality to be a social construct, and belief in God, he declared, a crutch for the intellectually challenged.

Much of the last decade of their friendship had been spent in debate over these issues. One would expect that such a vast difference in beliefs would drive a friendship apart, but for these two friends, it only drew them closer as they tried to save each other. Once a month, they met at a breakfast diner to enjoy each other's company and to continue their "conversation," as they called it. Today was one such morning.

Tristen looked to his left as a 2021 Jaguar pulled into the slot next to his with the driver blowing the horn. He smiled as Jake jumped from the vehicle and slapped the roof of his car, shouting at him, laughing good-naturedly.

"Yeah! That's right! I see your soccer-mom-mobile. Look with envy upon my chariot of power!"

Tristen smiled huge, shut off his engine, and got out of his vehicle.

Jake Evans, computer tech guru, had made his first million before the age of twenty-eight and was working on his tenth at thirty-three. He worked for one of the biggest tech companies in the US, and because of the success of some of his innovations, an article about him had appeared in "Modern Science Weekly." His career was skyrocketing and his personal life blooming. Jake's wife, Ilsa, cardiac surgeon and smoking hot, had given birth to their first child last month. Becka, to his mind, still looked somewhat like an alien with her wrinkly face and beady eyes, but, oh, how he did love her. She'd given purpose to his life and opened up a part of him that was still new.

Jake considered himself a self-made man, but the two women in his life challenged that proclamation. His self-touted views of family and their origins in the human instinct for self-propagation were no longer quite so strong. Not that he'd tell his best friend, Tristen, that. No, let Tristen believe his friend was still just as belligerently confident as he'd always been. Otherwise, he might find a crack to exploit at this morning's ritual.

Standing outside his car in the Denny's parking lot, Jake watched Tristen get out of his hideous van and smiled to himself. Tristen looked ridiculous. All of six feet, four inches and two hundred twenty pounds, with dark mahogany skin and movie star looks, Tristen looked like Chadwick Bozeman getting out of a Prius.

"Bro, you have *got* to get a new ride!" He laughed at Tristen as they met and embraced at the trunk of his Jag. Tristen laughed in return.

"Yeah, when the kids graduate." Tristen smiled. "Until then it's the ... what'd you call it? Oh yeah, the soccer-mom-mobile. Not all of us are millionaires like you, man."

Jake gave an "aw shucks" shrug.

"When you got it like that, you got it. Besides, Pastor Jordan, I'm sure the congregation would like to see a little more Creflo Dollar outta you."

"Whoa! Not cool!" Tristen laughed. "How about TD Jakes?"

"Okay, Jakes, whatever."

"I don't know if I could fit in your tiny Jag anyway. Since when did they start making luxury cars in dwarf size?" Tristen stood to his full height and not so discreetly shouldered up to his friend.

At five foot two and a hundred twenty pounds soaking wet, Jake's diminutive size was an easy target.

"Dang, bro, that was low ... no pun intended."

The friends shared a laugh. "That's for the Creflo Dollar quip you just shot at me."

"Okay, truce." Jake raised his hands in surrender. "We gonna eat or stand out here wasting daylight? I'm hungry."

"Yeah, me too. Let's eat."

The interior of the restaurant was warm and inviting. The large dining area hummed with the murmur of conversation, the musical sound of dishes being shifted, and sunlight flowing through the bay windows. Servers weaved through tables distributing food and drink along with warm smiles and kind words. The customers ensconced in the comfortable atmosphere enjoyed the company of their friends and loved ones while filling up on warm food and coffee. It was everything a beautiful Saturday morning in spring should be.

Tristen and Jake sequestered themselves in their usual corner booth within the restaurant's pocket of humanity and were eventually surrounded by mostly empty plates while their "conversation" heated up. A pair of bikers obviously fighting off a late night's libations were seated at a table to their left, trying to act like they weren't listening in on the discussion. In the booth next to them was a single mother with her small boy, who had earlier engaged Tristen in a vicious game of rock, paper, scissors until his mother had intervened with a smile and a quiet apology. Tristen and the boy, Matthew, had grinned at each other and kept at it until Tristen's food arrived.

Jake was now ranting on about God's supposed existence and the complete lack of evidence for such a belief. It was a familiar line of attack, and as Tristen focused in on his friend's point, he almost spit eggs as he guffawed.

"What?" Jake asked, with a surprised look. "Nietzsche was a genius before his time. His concepts on morality and God were revolutionary. He may be the only atheist whose ideas became common phrases we still use today. 'Survival of the fittest,' heard of that? That was him."

"Oh." Tristen swallowed his eggs and set down his fork with a smile. "Are we measuring the legitimacy of our points by the sayings our respective teachers coined?

How about the Golden Rule, or 'an eye for an eye,' or 'seek and you shall find,' or any other of the myriad sayings Christianity made popular?"

"We-ell ..." Jake laughed and tried to backpedal, but Tristen gave him no time before continuing.

"And why is it Nietzsche is so highly regarded by atheists?" Tristen mimed looking genuinely confused as he hammered home his point. "The man died in an insane asylum ravaged by syphilis, a disease he acknowledged getting from a prostitute, mind you, and being cared for by his mother, a Christian. It is said he spent his last years babbling Bible verses. Jake, that sure does sound like a ... what did you call him? Oh yeah, a genius."

"How a man died doesn't invalidate what he did while he was alive," Jake rebutted. He took a sip of coffee before continuing. "He still made valid points on the existence of God and the need for God as a societal crutch."

"Granted," Tristen acquiesced, "the end of his life doesn't totally invalidate his work, but it does factor into the veracity one should give it." Jake nodded in agreement. "Besides, I can prove to you in minutes what Nietzsche spent his whole life trying to disprove."

Jake hooted.

"This'll be rich!" He leaned into the table. "You are telling me that in mere minutes, you'll what, tear down theory that is still studied today? Be specific."

Tristen leaned back with a gleam in his eye. "Let's not take on every point that your idol tried to make. How about we start with one and see where that takes us?"

"And that one point is?" Jake asked suspiciously.

"Why, the existence of God, of course. In a few quick moments, we'll lay the groundwork for the absolute need for a Creator." Tristen drummed his fingers on the table nonchalantly. "I mean, if you got the time."

Jake laughed at his friend's boast. Tristen was normally all humility and reasonableness. He'd make him pay for his boasting.

"Really? Just a few moments of my time?" Jake asked with feigned innocence.

"Yep," Tristen said.

"Well, let's see if we can get some witnesses."

Jake rapped his fist firmly on their table. Dishes jumped. Silverware rattled loudly. The bikers at the next table looked grimly at him, and a passing waitress stopped mid-stride.

"Excuse me, patrons, sorry for the ruckus, but my friend the incomparable Pastor Tristen Jordan is about to prove to us the very existence of God!"

The waitress cocked an eyebrow with dubious interest. "Really?"

"Oh, yes!" Jake confirmed with a smile. "And in only minutes."

"So what?" one of the bikers snarled.

His companion punched him. "Nah, hold up, Wally. I gotta hear this." The second biker's leather vest sported a nametag that read *J.W.* "Care to put your money where your mouth is, Pastor?"

Jake prodded his friend. "Yeah, ante up."

Tristen, not one to be cowed by an audience, reached into his pocket and pulled out his wallet. He drew out a bill, then replaced the wallet in his pocket.

"All right. With this hundred-dollar bill, we'll produce reasonable evidence that there is a God." He looked at the first biker. "What's your name?"

The grumpy biker set down his fork and scowled. "Wally."

"Would you hold this, Wally?" Tristen gave him the bill. "If you're not satisfied in two minutes that there is a God, then you're a hundred dollars richer."

"I can deal with that." Wally smirked as he began to fold the bill up, but he was interrupted by Tristen's earnest question.

"Let me ask you a simple question, Wally." Tristen paused for effect. "How did that bill come into existence?"

The biker looked confused. "What?"

"The hundred-dollar bill. How did it come into existence?" Tristen gently reiterated.

"Uh, somebody made it."

"Really?" Tristen curiously asked. "How do you know it didn't slowly, over a few billion years, manifest itself out of a pile of linen fibers and then fall into a puddle of ink to get that arrangement of characters on it?"

"That's ridiculous!" Wally's face wrinkled in disgust. The waitress who'd been listening intently jumped in and snatched the bill from the biker.

"Look at it!" She snapped the bill between her hands. "It's clearly been designed by someone. There's writing and numbers all over it."

Tristen leaned forward expectantly. "Designed, you say?"

"Uh, *yeah*," the waitress said, with more than a touch of sarcasm.

Jake groaned from his seat, knowing where this was going and knowing he was unable to rebut.

"Would you agree, Wally?" Tristen asked the biker.

"Of course."

"Okay. Then would you agree that the human body is a lot more intricate in its design than a simple hundred-dollar bill?"

The confusion on the biker's and waitress's faces was clear. The biker responded slowly.

"Well ..."

"Within your body are some of the most mystifying designs known to man," Tristen quietly said. "Your digestive system is a miraculous balance of chemical breakdown and energy production. Your heart, Wally? Scientists can't tell you why it beats. They know how it does but are stumped as to why. Or your brain. The human brain is so intricate that doctors have only the most basic knowledge of its function."

The biker looked at the bill in his hands. "Huh."

Tristen said gently, "So, Wally, how did you come into existence?" The biker looked at Tristen curiously while he continued. "If a hundred-dollar bill by its existence proves it was designed by someone, then by that same reasoning, your very existence, your much more *complicated* existence, proves that you were designed by someone—God."

The waitress laughed and walked off. Wally looked shell-shocked, and his friend slapped his back. Jake had his head in his hands, but Tristen was still focused on Wally, who was working through the implications of their conversation. Wally handed the bill back to Tristen.

"But what about evolution?" Wally said. "I thought we evolved from monkeys."

Jake took the opportunity to insert himself back into the conversation. Someone had to save the situation. "Don't even get him started on that, Wally. He says it's a bedtime story."

Both bikers looked at Tristen, who was laughing. The small boy in the booth next door was standing on his seat smiling. Tristen looked at him with mock sincerity. "Whoa! I never said that!"

The boy giggled at Tristen.

"No?" Jake questioned Tristen, who equivocated.

"Well, not that I recall."

"You called evolution a myth, a fairy tale conjured up by the atheistic movement to instill fear and doubt into the believing masses."

Tristen acknowledged Jake's point with a wink. "Yeah, that does sound like me."

"Yes, it does." Jake's ire was beginning to show. "Then you went on to say that not only is there no proof or evidence to support Darwinian evolution but even Darwin himself had his doubts about the theory."

"That's because there isn't! And he did!" Tristen leaned forward on the table, his own ire rising now. "Every instance of supposed evidence, and I do mean every instance, has been proven to be false. Whether it was a pig's tooth dressed up as a human tooth, or the bones of a primate mistaken for those of a man. Every so-called 'discovery' has been debunked."

Jake exhaled loudly and shook his head. The other patrons had taken a backseat in this heavyweight duel. Tristen continued to hammer home his points.

"Bro." The passion oozed around every word Tristen formed. "Have you ever studied Darwin? Not his theory, but the man? He was a hack who even admitted, himself, that if his theory—stress on the word *theory*—was correct, then the world became an endless cycle of pointless existence. It was the atheistic movement that hijacked his theory and sold it as fact."

Jake could remain silent no longer.

"Life *is* a pointless existence!"

"I disagree." Disappointment edged Tristen's voice.

"Look around you, Pastor." Jake's eyes narrowed in challenge. "Evil runs rampant every day. And good is becoming—no, has become—a reality that fewer and fewer people know. School shootings, race wars, hundreds dead every year on the streets of Chicago. Police murdering unarmed Blacks—it goes on and on. Where is your God in that? At least from my point of view, I can pursue my own definition of purpose and happiness without the worry of disgruntling some bully in the sky. A bully that, if he exists, lets the weak be trampled and the innocent be killed."

"Huh, your definition?" Tristen leaned back and took a sip of coffee while Jake spoke.

"Yeah, mine. I'm here, God's not."

"Really." Tristen set down his cup, his eyes fierce. "Why is it that when something good happens, it's the result of our own making, but when tragedy strikes, we rail against evil and shake our fists at the sky?"

"Because we've been sold a lie! Open your eyes!"

"Mine are wide open. I suggest we have it backward."

"In what way?" Jake's skepticism was shared by the bikers, who by their head shakes threw their lot in with him. Tristen acknowledged them with eye contact while answering.

"Instead of congratulating ourselves for our 'goodness' and accusing God of his wrong, we should be thanking God when we experience good and taking a hard look in the mirror when evil crashes our party."

"So, God gets all of the credit and none of the blame?" Jake's questions continued. "And we get none of the credit and all of the blame? Seems biased to me. I don't know about you."

The bikers rumbled their assent.

"Scripture tells us—" Tristen began.

"Here we go, boys!" Jake interrupted. Tristen persisted.

"Scripture tells us every good and perfect gift comes from above. Think about that honestly. How many times have you received good and knew in your heart you didn't deserve it?"

"Zero!"

"Really, Jake?" Tristen locked eyes with his friend. "So, when you looked into your daughter's eyes the day she was born, you felt you deserved that blessing? Or when your beautiful wife said 'I do,' you weren't feeling unworthy of her devotion? I remember when you got that promotion at work that you'd been wanting, but just that weekend you went to Vegas and—"

Jake hastily cut in. "I don't want to talk about that."

"Exactly. We never do, because then we realize the good in our lives is not only undeserved but to the contrary, it's actually unjust."

"Unjust?" Jake's voice was edged in exasperation. "I'll tell you what is unjust ..."

"Please do."

Picking up his fork, Jake used it to stab his points home.

"How many untold millions have been killed—no, murdered—in the name of God? A God they knew nothing of and had no desire to know!"

Tristen's only response was a sad nod of his head.

"Exactly!" Jake said. "Religion is a tool used by a corrupt power structure to control the masses. And when those millions are killed in their holy wars, it is dismissed as God's judgment. From the Christian crusades to the Muslim jihads, slaughter has crossed the globe. And to this day, Muslim jihadists blow themselves up and go on rampages, and then the West retaliates by dropping more bombs. In the meantime, thousands are dying without so much as a teardrop shed by their killers, because they consider themselves doing their god's will."

"I admit that we theists have blood on our hands," Tristen agreed reluctantly.

"How magnanimous of you! Of course you do!"

"But how about atheism?" Tristen challenged.

Jake gave him a sardonic look. "What about us?"

"Hitler, Stalin, Pol Pot. Three men, just three, who studied atheistic teachings and applied those values to their lives. And the results, my friend? Hitler killed six million Jews on his way to building his master race. In World War II, more than fifty million people died, Stalin killed fifteen million more of his own people, conservatively, in his nihilistic attempt to purge Russia of undesirables. And Pol Pot? We're not even sure of his numbers, but we can be sure it's in the millions." Tristen paused to let the numbers sink in, then continued. "Just these three men killed more in their slaughters than all of the people who died in all of the Crusades combined."

"That's not atheism," Jake replied lamely. Even the bikers now seemed reluctant to join in.

"No?" Tristen sat back instead of jumping on his friend. The silence stretched uncomfortably. "So quick to shake your fist at heaven, but so reluctant to look in the mirror. But I offer this."

Jake groaned loudly. "What now?"

"The difference between Christian-related killings and atheistic killings."

"Which is?"

Tristen spoke slowly, laying down each word gently.

"When a Christian kills in the name of God, he is acting against his faith, not with it. His actions do not portray the will of God. They actually betray the God he claims to serve."

"And the atheist?" J.W. jumped in, curious.

"When an atheist kills, he is acting in concert with his belief system. With a moral baseline that is self-defined and an existence that has no ultimate meaning, the value of life becomes of no consequence, and the person with their finger on the trigger becomes the arbiter of his victim's worth. For better, or usually, for worse." Tristen concluded his argument with eye contact all around.

Jake, unwilling to lose, spoke into the group. "Christianity has all the answers, doesn't it?"

"No," Tristen admitted. "But we have the truth."

"And yet this truth gives no protection in a world full of evil and leaves its faithful no offer of full understanding."

"It leaves us something better."

"Better than exemption from tragedy or fear or death?" scoffed Jake. "Better than knowing exactly who, what, when, and why? Ha! I challenge you to give me something better than those things."

Tristen nodded his head in agreement as he answered. "Hope, Jake. It gives us hope. Hope for a better world, a better life, a better future. Not pointless existence. Hope."

Silence descended again as each man pondered what had been said. Instead of the moment becoming awkward, something powerfully spiritual moved among the group. The sarcasm, adversity and animosity bled away and were replaced by camaraderie. Even Jake was lost in introspection.

Finally, Wally broke the silence. "Hope? Huh."

"Yeah, I know, right?" Tristen commiserated. "It seems—"

Ding, ding.

The bell over the entrance chimed as two men entered wearing heavy coats.

"Look at these yahoos," Jake quipped while nodding in their direction. "Someone needs to tell them it ain't wintertime anymore. They could've left their coats at home."

Tristen and the bikers looked over. The two men entering the building looked grim, and the coats were suspicious.

"I don't want to be that person—" Jake said, as the two newcomers pulled guns from inside their coats. "Oh, *heck* no!"

One of the newcomers bellowed.

"Everybody down! Hit the floor!"

Taz pulled deeply on his best friend. That was what he called his crack pipe, his best friend. The narcotic smoke filled his lungs as he sucked in the numbing ecstasy. Holding his breath, he laid his head back on the headrest and shut his eyes. As the hit crested, he slowly let out his breath and let the tingling sensation travel down his body. He began cackling softly to himself until it turned into a full-out belly laugh.

"Toot! Toot!" he shouted gleefully, his voice reverberating in the enclosed space of the car. "All aboard the—I don't-give-a-what train! Next stop, dolla bills!"

His partner, Loco, listened to his antics with a twisted smirk on his face. "Get yo' mind right, homie." Readying the gun in his lap, he continued. "I don't need ya losin' ya mind when we hit this lick."

Taz looked at his partner with a wicked grin.

"No worries, G. I got ya." He pulled on the crack pipe again. "This is just the pick me up befo' I put it down. Ya wanna hit? Itta loosen ya up."

"Nah, head, let's just get this done." Loco put his gun in his waistband and zipped up his coat.

"Yeah, whateva. Let's do this." Taz set the crack pipe in the ashtray and grabbed his pistol from under the seat. He jammed the gun in his pants and exited the car, followed by Loco.

The partners approached the Denny's front doors quickly. Taz didn't know why they chose this place. He just followed his partner and waved his gun around when told to. One place was as good as another in his mind. Denny's, IHOP, Q-Trip ... First Baptist Church for all he cared. *Just keep me high and I'm in*, he thought to himself, and cackled softly.

His partner eyed him. "Hold it together."

The men entered the restaurant and took in the scene. About fifteen customers and a register, perfect. They pulled heat.

"Everybody down! Hit the floor!" Loco bellowed.

The stunned diners looked frozen, so Taz helped them out by shooting into the ceiling. "You heard 'im. Face down! Whatya waiting for?"

There was a bustle of activity as the diners all scrambled to the floor. The lone waitress behind the counter stood quivering, unsure of what to do. Loco turned to her and put his gun in her face.

"Open the register," he growled. The waitress just cried harder. "You have three seconds. One ... two ..." The waitress snapped out of it and hurriedly started pulling bills out of the register. "In the bag, lady. Taz?"

"What up, G?" The excitement was getting to Taz, whose high was peaking.

"Get these fools' wallets and cell phones. We don't need nobody live-tweeting this."

Taz laughed diabolically as he obeyed. "I got ya, homie."

While Loco collected money from the register, Taz made his way around the restaurant collecting money and phones. The diners all hurried to dump their belongings into the dirty pillowcase he held. He approached a table with a woman and child and collected her purse and phone. The four men lying on the floor had already piled their stuff in front of them. He'd have to watch these bikers. *They big as mountains,* he thought as he collected their things.

The small white man didn't have anything in front of him but a credit card.

"Hey, mini-me, where's your cellphone and wallet?" he asked dangerously, kneeling to put his gun against the man's head. "Where it at?"

"I don't have either on me!" the man claimed.

"What? Don't give me that!" Taz cocked his gun and pressed harder. "You got one mo' chance, then I'ma gonna ..."

"No, please, I swear!" the man begged.

The little boy in the booth started to wail.

"Hey, Taz!" Loco hollered from the front of the place. "Shut that kid up. It's getting on my nerves!"

Taz got up and quickly went to the booth.

"Shut up, kid!" He swung his gun to pistol-whip the boy, but his mother jumped in the way and fell back on top of the kid. The wailing stopped.

"Thank God! That was driving me—" Loco appeared at his partner's side with his sack of cash. "Now who else is jabbering?"

The two gunmen looked and saw the white man huddled on the floor mumbling to himself. Taz laughed and kneeled in front of him, tapping his gun on his head.

"What ya sayin', white boy?"

The mumbling got louder. "Please God, if you let me live, I'll never doubt you again. Just let me out of this, and I swear I'm yours."

Taz couldn't help himself. "I'm high as a kite, and this white boy prayin'?"

The mumbled prayer continued.

"Kill that fool," Loco growled.

"Got ya." Taz stood up and took aim.

Click!

"Holy spit! A misfire? Don't matter." He cocked his weapon again after clearing out the bunk shell. "I got all day."

Sirens erupted outside the building. The two criminals looked up in panic.

"Let's go, G!" Taz yelled. Loco jumped for the door with Taz hot on his trail. They burst from the restaurant, firing their weapons. The police in the parking lot opened fire, and the bullets rained into the men. Their bodies jerked spasmodically and then collapsed onto the concrete.

The last thing Taz thought was *this is knocking my high*.

Jake's whole world was in a muddle. He felt as if time had slowed down in the restaurant. Seconds passed by like minutes as his brain tried feebly to catch up. He could hear a female customer screaming, but her words didn't register. He heard Tristen call out and saw him scramble past. It was like a dream sequence in some movie, all out of sync and unreal. Rolling onto his hands and knees, he tried to focus his mind on what had just happened. His limbs trembled as they obeyed.

What happened? He sat back slowly on his haunches, time still in slow motion. He had been mere seconds from death. He'd looked down the barrel of his extinction and the hammer had fallen. The click of the misfire seemed like an auditory hallucination, but it wasn't. Why? Why wasn't he dead? The prayer. He remembered praying to a God he'd never truly believed in ... and God had answered.

"Oh, my God." The words slipped from his mouth, and reality snapped back into full swing.

Jake found himself kneeling among pandemonium. The gunfire outside the restaurant was ending. Stray bullets had shattered the glass in one of the building's windows. The bikers were getting to their feet stoically, and the waitress behind the counter was screaming into the phone. Something about an ambulance.

"My baby!" The single mother—Valerie?—was hysterical. "Please save him! He's not breathing!"

The boy lay on the floor with Tristan kneeling over him doing chest compressions. Jake got up hurriedly and went to his friend.

"Come on, kid," Tristen begged as he worked. "Breathe. Father, don't let him die."

Another minute went by, and it was obvious to everyone, including the quietly sobbing mother, that the boy's fight was done. Tristen kept pumping on his chest.

"It's over, Preacher." The biker Wally spoke softly. "Look at his neck."

The little boy's neck was at an unnatural angle. Jake put his hand on Tristen's shoulder.

"He's gone, Tris."

The gentle words and touch seemed to break Tristen. He sat back on his haunches as the mother picked up her child, cradling him while she sobbed.

A half hour later, the two friends sitting quietly on the curb outside the Denny's had been interviewed by the police and told they could go. Jake looked at his friend who was so obviously shell-shocked. He knew Tristen was struggling and thought he could stand to hear some good news. Jake had prayed, and God had answered! He didn't know exactly what that meant, but he knew that his days of doubt were over. That was a fact. He went to speak, but before he could, Tristen spoke into the silence.

"Where was he?" Tristen asked quietly.

"Who?"

"God." The sadness in Tristen bellowed forth in that one quiet word. "I don't understand."

"Did you see what happened?" Jake asked.

"Huh? What?" Something sparked in Tristen's eyes.

"That guy," Jake stammered uncertainly. "He tried to kill me ... but I prayed and the gun ... it didn't go off. God must've—"

"Don't you dare!" his friend furiously hissed. "That kid just died in my arms!" The anger morphed into something new inside the well-intentioned pastor. "I prayed too!" He was breathing hard, nostrils flared. "Where ... oh Lord ... were you?"

"But ..." Jake was shocked by what he was hearing. "You said that ..."

"I don't want to hear it!" his friend shouted as he surged to his feet.

"Wait!" Jake rose to his feet, only to watch his best friend storm off. Tristen jumped into his van, gunned the engine, and barreled out of the parking lot, leaving his faith behind in a cloud of burned rubber. Jake was left standing there in utter confusion.

"But ... I prayed," he said quietly.

CHAPTER 7

BUTTERFLY TRILOGY, PART 2: LOVE HARD

The sun hung high in the sky, burning with the intensity of a refiner's fire. Its rays slowly baked everything on the surface of the earth, including the man slowly trudging his way through the desert dunes. One dune after another was an endless journey, from where, he did not know, and *to* where, he wasn't quite sure either. Yet he continued with a purposeful stride, unyielding to, and almost bolstered by, the sun's unrelenting pressure upon his skin.

It had been a while since he'd seen anything but sand, the last time being his amazing trek into "the oasis," as he'd named it. There he had drunk deeply from the waters that still, weeks later, slaked his thirst. He didn't know how this was possible, but his unflagging energy attested to it. The memory of the oasis's cool pond, lush grass, birdsong, and tall trees was giving him energy. He would have thought himself insane if not for the one thing that evidenced his journey more than anything. There to his right, fluttering on the air currents a few feet away, was his new companion.

The butterfly stopped when he did and seemed to lock eyes with him. No, this was no optical illusion, it was absolutely looking at him. The man no longer denied the situation, but it still awed him. The butterfly flitted closer and landed on its favorite perch—his nose. The man stifled a sneeze and laughed softly.

"Hello there, Lily," he said to his friend.

He had no idea if this was the butterfly's name. Probably not, but he thought it a whimsical name that fit her perfectly. As usual, when he spoke to the butterfly, its response came in the sound of musical chiming on the wind. The beautiful sound seemed to speak directly to his soul, and he immediately felt at peace.

"Yes," he replied, "we should rest now."

At that exact moment a shadow covered them, and the sun's heat abruptly dissipated. The man looked up, and to his complete shock, there, hanging in the sky directly above them, was a fat cloud. The man gave a joyous shout, and the butterfly took flight and flew a pattern of celebration.

The man collapsed in the rapidly cooling sand and lay spreadeagled with his eyes on the sky and the cloud hovering there. He felt a slight tingle on his right index finger that told him his friend was with him. He turned his head and looked at the beautiful creature with its ever-changing, multi-colored wings flexing rhythmically, its antennae dancing. The man felt a burning love well up inside him.

"I know you're only a butterfly now," he whispered through a constricting throat, "but I also know how your lips feel on mine. The sight of your beauty, the whisper of your spirit, and the glimpse of forever in your eyes has entwined my heart with yours. I pray for the day I can look on your face without this desert all around us."

The sound of music filled his ears, and the man knew the butterfly had understood him and felt the same. He closed his eyes and was soon in a daze of half-sleep. He dreamed of cool waters, of chasing someone through a glade of green grasses and beautiful flowers. They laughed and chased each other, her laughter like the sound of the joy of music. He murmured her name in his sleep.

Buzzing like staccato thunder sounded in his ears. A few seconds later, the loud, ominous buzzing passed his ears again, and his eyes popped open. When his eyes opened, the knowledge of what that sound was came instantly to his mind—dragonfly.

"Lily!" he cried out.

The man sat bolt upright, sheer panic running through his veins. He looked frantically left and right, his eyes straining to find his friend, his companion, his love. A flicker of movement in the near distance caught his attention, and he could make out a butterfly flying a zigzag pattern of distress. Close behind was the dragonfly. Darting in, the predator narrowly missed its prey.

"*No!*" the man roared and jumped to his feet in a spray of sand.

The butterfly and dragonfly were only a short distance away. His feet pounded through the sand, his heart thundering in his chest as he closed in on them. He was only a few yards away when the dragonfly feinted right. The butterfly overcompensated, allowing the dragonfly to torpedo in and strike mid-air. They tumbled to the sand in a tangle of wings. The man's heart felt near to bursting as he closed the last few feet in a blind rage.

The dragonfly, on top of its quarry, sensed the man's approach and it flew into the air to escape, but it was too late. The man swatted the dragonfly to the ground and then fell upon it with his fists, hammering the sand in a blurring fury. With unmerciful blows he pounded the dragonfly into oblivion, until all that was left were bits of gelatinous mush.

With bruised knuckles, the man returned a few paces to the figure lying prone in the sand. Falling to his knees he looked down on the butterfly. He was scared to touch it because of the damage.

"Lily, no," he said painfully, as tears poured from his eyes.

The butterfly was terribly injured. One wing was almost completely sheared off, connected only by a slender sinew.

Its antennae were bent at odd angles and moved slowly, painfully. Two punctures in its body leaked fluid into the sand. The butterfly moved pitifully, breaking the man's heart and spirit. He reached down and carefully scooped up the battered butterfly.

"I'm sorry," he whispered into his hands, cradling his companion. "I should have been there."

The wind blew and on it floated broken musical notes, and he knew in his heart that the butterfly was trying to absolve him from guilt, even as it lay dying in his hands. That knowledge broke the man, and the tears flowed freely down his cheeks.

He didn't know how much time had passed, but the next time he came to his senses he was sitting on his haunches, rocking back and forth in grief. The movement from the butterfly had long since stopped. The man had no words to express his grief, no way to express the loss inside him. The love in his heart burned like an inferno, and he wanted it to consume him.

He focused on that fire in his chest, and to his relief it burned hotter. He thought to himself, *yes, burn me away,* as the flames inside spread. Soon the blaze was traveling down his legs and into his toes, spreading through the sands around. The sand started to shift and glow as its grains grew hotter and hotter.

The man expected this to be painful, but it was not, and soon the intense heat traveled down his arms and into his hands. He cupped the butterfly inside his hands and clenched his eyes shut as his lungs filled with heat. The love inside him was fanned to a crescendo, and the man, on utter instinct, lowered his lips to his hands. He breathed an unending breath of fiery air into his cupped fingers.

With all the love in him, he breathed. With all the energy his broken heart contained, he breathed. When he felt close to being tapped out, he loved harder and breathed. His hands started to glow with an ethereal luminescence, and the air around him started to shimmer. The light in his hands glowed so brightly that the man and the butterfly at its center were blotted out. Then, with a crack like lightning, everything in the man's sight went black, and he floated in nothingness.

Adrift in the inky darkness, the fire in his chest now gone, the man felt his sanity return. With it came the sound of songbirds, the brush of grass against his skin, and the gentle caress of a soft wind. He opened his eyes and found himself lying on his back in a meadow. Flowers bloomed all around, small colorful trees held boisterous birds, and a small brook flowed no more than a few feet from him. A diminutive doe had its nose in the water, and she regarded him without fear.

The man stood up and felt immediately as if he'd been in this place before. This place was distinctly different from the oasis he'd visited, yet the same. How was that? Before he could think any further, he felt a wet nuzzling on his hand. He looked down and saw the doe looking back up at him quizzically. Then it bounded away.

The smell of cherry blossoms on the breeze caused the man to start walking through the meadow. He had no thoughts on his mind but one. Where was Lily? Was she alive? He had to find her.

He walked through glade after glade without seeing her or anything living, except forest creatures. The animals all seemed oddly aware of his presence. He stopped a few feet from another deer and asked stupidly, "Can you take me to Lily?"

The deer looked at him and continued to chew the grass it had tugged from the meadow. It bent for another mouthful before walking away from him.

"Stupid animal!" the man said in frustration.

He walked over a fallen log with moss covering it and sat down. Tears began to slide down his cheeks as he thought of his loss. He couldn't believe he had lost her. Here he was in her land, and he couldn't share it with her.

He put his face in his hands and said to himself, "Take me back to the desert. I don't want to be here."

Just then a wind picked up and blew softly through the meadow. On the current carried the soft tones of a familiar tune. The man stood up quickly, straining his ears to listen. The wind blew harder, and the man caught the direction of the music. He took off sprinting.

Dodging trees, jumping small streams, and scaring unsuspecting wildlife, he bounded through the meadow. Stopping only to make sure that he was on the right track, he ran until he was sweating and breathing heavily. And still he ran.

The music got louder until he broke through a line of small trees and found himself in a clearing. He stopped abruptly and looked around. He was surrounded by tall trees. How had they appeared out of nowhere? One particularly large tree sat in the middle of the clearing. Its leaves were the strangest thing he'd ever seen, multicolored and changing colors as they moved.

He took a step closer, and the leaves seemed to explode from the tree. The man sat down heavily, startled as hundreds of butterflies took flight. They flew in hundreds of different directions and disappeared into the trees, leaving the man alone, and still music poured from the tree.

The man got to his feet and approached the tree slowly.

As he got closer, he noticed a large hollow in the tree. A glassy looking chrysalis or pod rested inside the hollow, and it was from there the music emanated. He walked up to the tree and put his hand on the crystalline surface, running his hand across it.

The music got louder. The cocoon-like thing was about shoulder high, so he bent over and put his cheek to it to listen intently. The warmth against his skin felt nice, but he couldn't hear any movement. He stood back up but left his hand on it.

Suddenly a hand slapped on the other side opposite his hand, startling him. The sight of the dainty hand on the inside of the pod made his heart beat hard with hope. Music like laughter floated from the chrysalis, and he knew immediately what he should do.

"Lily," he said softly.

At once, the glassy structure fell to pieces, its glittering shards falling onto the grass, leaving only the hollow and its shadowy depths. The man didn't know he was crying until he felt cool tears on his chest. Music issued forth again, and his tears stopped.

"Lily," he said again.

Out of the hollow stepped a familiar petite figure. Her long hair flowed and caught in the air. The small dress she wore clung to her lithe figure. She padded over to the man on bare feet and stopped in front of him where he stood staring in amazement. She wiped his still-wet tears from his cheeks and smiled.

He looked into her mystical eyes and was at a loss for words. The almond shape of her eyes and their ever-changing color mesmerized him. How could she be here? He had held her broken body in his own hands. He raised a hand and brushed her cheek lightly with his fingers. Her hand reached up and entwined her fingers with his.

This time it was she that leaned forward and kissed him boldly on the lips. The contact left him woozy. She giggled that amazing chime-like giggle.

"How?" he said.

"You," she stated matter-of-factly, staring into his eyes.

"I don't understand," he replied.

"You love hard, don't you?" She laughed softly.

Remembering the fire that had blazed in his chest, the man answered, "Yes, I do. But you were dead."

"Yes, I was," she agreed. "But you wouldn't let me be, so I live."

"I don't understand," he repeated.

She leaned in and kissed him again. "I was dead. You loved me. Now I live. Okay?"

"Okay," he agreed this time. "I love you."

"I know, silly." She laughed. "I love you too."

Then she jumped on him, and they tumbled in the grass, laughing together. They lay in the grass, kissing passionately and laughing loudly until they were spent. Then they held each other, neither wanting to let go.

Her head on his chest and his hand tangled in her hair, they whispered to each other.

"Don't ever leave me again," the man said.

"I won't ... Web," she said.

"What?"

"Web," Lily said. "It's what I call you."

"Why?"

"It's your name."

"It is?" he asked.

"What's my name?" Lily asked.

"Lily," came his instant reply.

"Okay," she said. "Yours is Web."

Web laughed with new purpose. He hadn't known his name before. It was a good feeling.

"I love you," he said into her eyes.

She laid her head back down on his chest. "Silly man."

They laid there for a long time, until both dozed lightly, two figures at peace wrapped in the cocoon of each other.

Lily woke on her perch looking down into the sleeping eyes of her companion, the silly man whose life she'd saved, and who had then filled her with life. She remembered him refusing to accept her loss, and then willing her back to life with his love. Web, her Web. Fate had brought them together, and she would travel with him wherever Fate ordained ... until they could be together bodily forever.

She laughed musically and played a tune to the man's spirit. "Wake up."

The man mumbled in his sleep but didn't move.

"I love you, Web. Wake up," she strummed lightly to his soul.

His eyes fluttered up and he focused on Lily perched on his nose. Her wings flexed beautifully, her antennae dancing on her head. She looked even more beautiful than before. The color of her wings was more vibrant, the twinkle of her music louder. Her graceful legs were longer too.

"You're even more mystifying now," he said, a smile on his face.

Lily took flight and fluttered above Web's head as he stood. The cool sand on his toes made him look up. The cloud was still there. The desert stretched out before them, dune after dune, but in the far-off distance, Web could make out what vaguely looked like mountains.

"Look," he said, pointing them out. Lily played a tune in response.

"Yes," Web agreed. "I think that's where we're going."

With that he started down the dune with new purpose. Lily fluttered over and landed on his right ear. Together they traveled toward the shapes in the distance. What lay ahead of them? How long would it take to get there? That lay unknown. But they had each other ... and for them, that was enough.

Above them, the cloud started to move with them.

TO BE CONTINUED ...

CHAPTER 8

THE EXTRATERRESTRIAL

As I entered the gymnasium, the noise of the crowd enveloped me, and the bustle of the packed building jostled me from side to side. Humanity pressed into me, and I almost fled right then. Why was I even here? Because some weird old lady had told me to come here? I didn't even know her. She could be some escaped mental patient. She sure seemed like it. All that crazy otherworldly talk and that look in her eyes of surreal confidence. No one's that confident. Yeah, she was insane, for sure. But then how'd she know those things about me? For that matter, how'd she know I'd even be there? On that bench, on a snowy night, all alone on an empty college campus?

It still all felt like a dream.

For hours I'd sat there on that bench staring at my phone and a series of texts that changed my life.

SARA: I'm pregnant.
ME: What?
SARA: I'm pregnant.
ME: u sure?

A picture appeared, a photo of a positive pregnancy test. My next words flew off my fingers before I knew they were moving.

ME: You're not keeping it, right?
SARA: IDK
ME: Sara, I'm not ready neither r u!
SARA: Jaxon ... I can't do this right now.

Eight texts changed my life.

After wandering aimlessly around the campus, I found myself hours later sitting on that park bench, covered in snowflakes, barely aware of my frozen fingertips. The only things going through my head were fear and confusion. I wasn't ready to be a father.

I loved Sara with my whole soul, but I couldn't be a dad. My parents would kill me. Sara's parents too. High school sweethearts who, at the first chance at independence, end up pregnant and starting a family? That would mean we'd have to get married. A husband and father? No way. The alternative? A visit to a quiet clinic and no one would ever know. A couple hundred bucks, it would be taken care of, then Sara and I would go back to our lives.

I didn't know if we *could* go back after that, with such a dark secret between us. Sure, Pastor called abortion murder, and I'd always agreed, but that was before. I have plans ... Sara does too. She wants to be a doctor. She couldn't do that with a kid. All I needed to do was convince Sara that this was the best option for us. For our futures. Painful, of course, but it was the only choice.

With that decision made, I sat back against the snowy bench and realized I wasn't alone. Sitting next to me silently was an older lady. She was dressed for the cold in a winter coat and a pair of thick mittens. Her salt-and-pepper hair sparkled with a dusting of snow, and the tip of her nose was chilled pink. Her breath plumed in front of her face as she looked off into the distance. Her posture was regal and the small smile she wore was disarming, but something about her was otherworldly. How had she sneaked up on me like that?

I must've been zoned out because she'd just appeared. I looked around the empty campus and saw no one else off in the distance. I could hear the noise from the gymnasium where a game was being played. Other than that, it was only us two.

The lady looked at me then, all quiet assurance, and greeted me like all of this wasn't completely nuts.

"Hello," she said with a smile. "It's cold out here."

"Yeah, uh, it is." I didn't know how to answer. *Duh—there's snow on the ground. Of course it's cold, lady!*

"I was headed to the game, but then I saw you sitting here." She said it as if it clearly explained why she'd approached a stranger on a darkened college campus and started a conversation. "You looked like you could use a distraction. Or maybe you'd like to tell me something?"

Her gentle prompt had triggered something in me, and I found myself replying, "I'm gonna be a dad."

"Really?" Her face brightened. "That's great news! Congratulations!"

"Well, I don't know if we'll keep it."

"Ah." She breathed deeply and looked away. "That's why I'm here."

Who the heck is this lady with her judgmental "Ah"?

"What's that supposed to mean?" I asked.

"I just felt led over here," she said softly.

"Led? By whom?"

She looked back at me with a wry grin and looked up at the sky, letting me draw my own conclusions.

"What? Aliens told you to come over here? You beam down from the mothership or something?"

Oblivious to the angry sarcasm in my voice, she merely looked over at me with genuine warmth and chuckled.

"Aliens? That's funny. No, not a mothership, but guidance from above. You see, I was on my way to the basketball game ... wait, I already said that, didn't I?"

"Yeah, you did."

89

She looked away again and sat quietly. Seconds ticked by before I prompted her.

"Sooo ...?"

"When is the right time to give up on someone?" she asked.

The non sequitur threw me, but I tried to keep up. "Uh, never?"

"That's right, Jaxon." She smiled at me warmly.

How does she know my name?

"Hey, how did you know my name?" I asked suspiciously. She gestured to my phone, with its screensaver with my name glowing in the night.

"Oh," I said quietly.

She laughed at my chagrin.

"Children."

I bristled. I thought she was talking about me before she continued.

"Children are the legacy in our lives that remind us of all the successes and mistakes we've made in life. As parents we look to them, and rightly or not, we measure ourselves against the backdrop of their lives. Every mistake they make feels like a condemnation of the job we did, and every success feels like an equal confirmation of the good in us.

"Sometimes there are moments when we want to give up on our children because the pain we feel for them is too raw. And there are times when our hearts feel like they'll burst with pride for the things they accomplish. It's always a feast or famine experience raising children. I know, not a ringing endorsement. Feast or famine, pain or pride, self-incrimination and self-congratulations? Who'd sign up for that?"

I agreed silently, nodding my head.

"But Jaxon, you know what?" she asked with a pointed look.

"What's that?"

"No parent, and I mean none, would ever wish they hadn't had the opportunity to love their child." The confidence in her tone was scary. "I don't care if you're the father of Jeffery Dahmer or Adolf Hitler, you wouldn't regret their life."

"You wouldn't?"

"No. We'd ask for another opportunity to raise them better. Another chance to be the mother or father they needed. Sometimes a child's life can be seen as a burden, or something to end before it begins because you'd be relieved of future grief. I know. I've been there."

I could see the pain etched onto her face. I couldn't help but ask, "You've had an abortion?"

"No," she said, with a small shake of her head. "But I've felt the grief you're feeling now. I was challenged to give up before the fight had even begun."

"But that's not the same thing," I argued, "if you haven't had an abortion."

"Isn't it? Isn't it the same?" This was the first time she looked near anger, but I quickly realized she was merely vexed. "Why is it we like to believe pain is so unique to our specific situation? If I slam my thumb in a door and you hit your thumb with a hammer, don't we both feel the same thing? Don't believe the lie that your pain and my pain are so different. Are they twin brothers? No, but cousins in the same family, surely. We are related through this pain and because of that relation we can help each other."

"Help each other what?"

She smiled at me like I was slow, and she was giving me time to catch up.

"You were the one sitting in the snow, out here in the dark, staring at your phone. Surely you needed help. Or at least a coat."

"What do I need help with? I've already decided," I snapped.

"Oh, so you've given up." She looked away but quickly looked back, and then reached over and patted my hand. "Can I show you something?"

Something in her voice made me wary. "I don't know."

She laughed at that. "Just come inside with me." She gestured to the gymnasium where the basketball game was being played. "It'll be warm, and you can watch the game while you decide. Or whatever it is you were doing."

She stood up and dusted the collected snow off her lap. I reluctantly stood, and she took that as confirmation that I'd be joining her.

Whatever. I ain't got nothing better to do than follow a crazy person around. It's either that or freeze. I let her lead me to the gym.

Which is how I ended up here in this hot, muggy gym being bumped to and fro by the packed crowd. My ears and nose started to burn as feeling returned to them, and I looked at the small woman beside me. She managed to find a crease in the press of bodies and was watching the action on the court with a rapt expression. She must have felt me watching, because she looked up and winked at me before pointing at the floor where the players battled.

"You're missing it," she said with a smile, and went back to watching the game,

What does this have to do with anything we've been speaking about?

I sighed and watched the game. In for a penny, in for a pound plus five dollars' change, right? *You follow a strange woman around, you can't complain when things get strange.*

I focused on the game which really was something to watch. The players moved beautifully on the court in a choreography of athleticism and strength. The ball zipped from one player to the next while the defenders tried valiantly to keep the ball from going into the basket. The squeak of rubber soles on the hardwood and the grunting of colliding athletes added to the symphony of action.

Add to that the almost perfectly in-tune *oohs* and *ahs* from the crowd, and when the ball went through the net, the orchestration crescendoed in cheers and boos.

I felt myself become lost in the majesty of the struggle as I noticed one player who was obviously better than everyone else. His movements were more fluid, his focus more intent, and the ball seemed to find him more often than not and invariably went into the net as he shot it or dunked it with ease. The crowd was seeing what I was and began to chant his name.

"Fred-dy! *Fred-dy*!" The ball found his hands off a rebound, and he caught it and dribbled the length of the court like a ballet dancer. He weaved and twisted effortlessly, then took flight from an impossible distance and slammed the ball home. A defender was knocked to the floor after having jumped to block the shot. This paragon of athletic prowess dropped from the rim and went straight to the defender. The star helped the embarrassed opponent from the ground with a smile and patted his back.

"Good ups, bro!" he encouraged. "You got skills. Let's go. Ball up."

The defender straightened up and seemed to stand taller. The game resumed, only to be cut short by the sounding buzzer. The third quarter was over, and the teams went to their benches.

I'd been so focused on the game I'd forgotten about my escort. I looked to my side, but she was gone. Confused, I looked around but couldn't see the woman anywhere. I turned in a circle trying to spot her salt-and-pepper hair bobbing in the crowd. No luck. She was gone.

"You have to be kidding me!" I grumbled loudly, and the man next to me looked at me in challenge. "No, not you. My bad."

Angry now, I turned to leave this stupid gym. *That's what I get for coming in here.* Just as I turned, I heard someone calling my name.

"Jaxon! Jaxon! Yo, over here!"

I looked over to see a group of my friends also in attendance. Wheeler, the one who yelled my name, was waving at me wildly, trying to get my attention. He stood with Allen and Kai who saluted me with their drinks. The only thing to do was go over to them and say "what's up" before I left. If not, Wheeler would track me down to see what was bothering me, and after the crazy lady, I was not down for another conversation about that.

I moved graceless through the crowd, trying to not step on any toes while I passed. It was a losing strategy, and I was bombarded with dirty looks and jostled roughly for my impudence. Crowds. I hate crowds.

"What's up, y'all?" I greeted my friends. There were fist-bumps and half-hugs around as we acknowledged one another.

"What are you doing over there all by yourself?" Wheels asked. "And where's your girl?"

Wheeler had always been the adult of our group. Annoying, yes, but it was also why we loved him.

"Ah, I just stopped in to check out the game," I said. "I didn't know it was gonna be so cold."

"It's winter, bro," Allen said, like I was an idiot. Which I understandably looked like. Allen was our resident smart aleck, so his sarcasm was thick.

"Actually, it's still fall for another few days," Kai said as he pushed his glasses up on his face. He was the group brain, always chiming in with some tidbit of information.

Allen shot him an eyebrow. "Where I come from, snow equals winter."

"Yeah. Well, in fact, winter starts on a certain date each year," Kai lectured, "and that day is next week."

"He's got you there," Wheeler said with a smirk.

The conversation devolved into banter as my friends exchanged verbal darts and jabs. After a few minutes went by, I almost forgot my problems, and then the fourth quarter began.

The players traveled seamlessly up and down the floor with Freddy doing all the scoring again. It really was awe-inspiring to watch.

"Can you believe he's even here?" Kai asked me. I had no idea what he was talking about.

"Whatchya mean?" I responded.

"Freddy Aives." He nodded to the star who'd just knocked down a three-point shot and was trotting back up the court. "That dude should be in the ground."

"Huh?"

Wheeler jumped in at my obvious confusion. "Bro, that's the dude who fell off Woodmen Tower. Over a hundred floors, splat!"

"Ain't no way." The incredulity dripped from my lips. "You're telling me that dude, the one who just dropped that no-look dime, fell from a hundred floors and is still walking around?"

Allen looked at me skeptically. "You're telling me you didn't hear about that?"

"Of course, I heard about someone falling from that building, but I figured he was dead."

"Nah," Wheeler responded. "He should be, but he ain't. I mean falling from that height should've done him in."

"How'd he even fall?" I asked as I struggled to understand what I was hearing.

"He was at some frat party, drunk and high, of course, and they say he just jumped. They say he hit the ground so hard he broke into pieces!"

"Okay, now I know this is crazy." I looked between my friends, waiting for the punchline. "Y'all are serious?"

"Man," Allen jumped back in, "Kai was there! He seen it all. Tell him, bro."

Kai ran a hand through his shaggy hair and pushed his glasses up on his face again before speaking.

"I got there after the police arrived. The sidewalk was all taped off and even the news was there. Everyone was talking about it still, and the body was covered … well, it was covered in a few spots, cuz it wasn't exactly in one piece."

"Then how … ?" I looked to the floor where the dead man had just caught an alley-oop and slammed it home.

"This elderly lady comes out of nowhere," Kai continued. "She ducks under the tape, tears pouring down her face. She starts picking up the pieces. She's mumbling under her breath. The whole time the cops are telling her to stop and trying to get her to leave the scene."

My skin tingled in recognition. *An old lady?*

"The news turn their cameras on her, and people are starting to laugh and jeer. She passes where I am standing while she is picking up a foot, and I hear her say something like, 'It's not over,' and then she is past me."

"Impossible!" I broke in.

"Shut up and listen, bro," Allen quipped. He was obviously into the story. "It's gonna get crazier."

"Where was I?" Kai gathered his thoughts before continuing. "So, she gathers all the pieces and puts them together under the same sheet and then just kneels there mumbling. The cops, bro, they were flipping out. You got this little old lady walking around like she owns the place, picking up pieces of a person and ignoring their commands to stop. I don't know why they didn't Taser her. We were all waiting for it, but it was like they couldn't touch her."

"Then what happened?" I asked, spellbound. I needed to know how this ended.

"The coroner shows up and loads the body into a bag and into his van. The lady just sits there with her hands stretched out toward them as they did their work, all the while still mumbling. The coroner finishes loading up and goes to start the van, but it won't turn over. Suddenly, a bright light fills the back of the van. Bro, it was the eeriest stuff you ever saw!"

"Man, like some X-Files episode!" Allen said in awe.

"Exactly, bro," Kai agreed.

I'm dumbfounded. This can't be real.

"Well, this light gets so bright that you can't even see anymore, and I had to look away. People are scared, some are running, but most of them just freeze in place. When the light fades out, there are noises and shouts in the back of the van. The doors open and the coroner is waving over a paramedic who was still on the scene talking with the cops. They run over there, and next thing you know, one cop is drawing a weapon, another has fallen to his knees, and the paramedic is just standing there."

The crowd erupted as something exciting happened on the court, and I remembered to breathe. No one in our group was watching the game any longer.

"After a few minutes of loud talking, that guy," Kai gestured to the basketball floor and to Freddy Aives, "that guy gets out of the van like he wasn't just dead minutes before."

"Everybody there is silent. Not one word is spoken as the paramedics lead him to the ambulance. The news people snap out of it first and try to get to the ambulance, but it pulls away before they get to it. The cops leave and then the news people, but all us kids just stood around for hours talking. No one had any answers. Just crazy ideas about what we'd seen."

"The old lady," I asked quietly. "What happened to her?"

Kai looked confused like he never thought about that before. "You know, I don't know. She was just gone after that."

"What do you mean, just gone? That doesn't make any sense."

"Bro, a dead man came back to life," Kai exclaimed. "*None* of it makes any sense."

"The police and news are saying it was a hoax," Wheeler told us. "They think it was some elaborate college prank, and they tried to file charges on Freddy, but there were too many witnesses who saw what Kai saw."

"It was no hoax, bro," Kai assured us. "I don't know what happened, but it *happened*."

My gut churned as I digested what I just heard. A dead man coming back to life? A little old lady showing up at that exact moment? What did it mean? I needed some air.

"Hey, y'all, I'm 'bout to go. I have an assignment due tomorrow," I lied.

I said my goodbyes and made my way out of the gym. On my way out, the crowd seemed to part. I was so lost in thought I didn't even notice the lack of bumps and curses. I exited the building into the cold and began the long walk back across the campus to my dorm.

The frigid air burned my cheeks, and my fingertips tingled as I scrolled through my phone looking at the night's earlier texts. I needed to call Sara and talk through things. I knew I'd made a mess of the situation, and I wanted to be able to fix it. She deserved better from me ... our child deserved better.

"So. Still giving up?" The voice came from my left, and I looked to see the bench with a familiar old lady. In her downy winter coat and ridiculous mittens, she was the epitome of innocence, but I knew there was more to her than met the eye. Her face still had that wry smile like she knew what I was thinking. She patted the bench in invitation. "Have a seat."

I walked over but stayed standing. "I'm good here."

"Suit yourself," she said with a shrug. She gestured toward my phone with a nod. "You didn't answer my question."

"What?" I asked.

"Are you giving up?" She restated her loaded question.

"You're his mom, aren't you?" I asked, trying to catch her off guard. "Freddy, he's your son, right?"

"Yes," she agreed with a smile. "He's my son. I love him with all my heart. Did you see him in there? His gift is amazing."

I sat down on the bench. "Yeah, I saw him …
friends told me about his … uh … accident. About how he almost died."

"It was a close thing." She nodded. "But it's not over till it's over, and it wasn't his time yet."

So many questions jumped into my mind, but I asked the broadest, most incredulous one.

"What happened?"

"I never gave up," she replied, like it was that simple.

"Huh?"

"Jaxon, there comes a time in every parent's life where we can give up on our children. There will be situations where all seems to be lost, that all hope has fled, but in those moments we must never fold. People around you will try to convince you. They'll tell everyone around them that your child is lost." She looked at me intently until she knew I heard her. "Don't believe them. You are going to be a father. No, you *are* a father. Right now, your job begins. Don't give up on your child before its life even begins."

"But what about—" I tried to ask, but she cut me off.

"Whatever you're about to ask doesn't mean anything. If you start to run down the 'what-if' road, you'll get lost in what's already lost and lose your way even further." She saw the look of confusion on my face and clarified. "Most people, when faced with something like what you're facing, will either live in the past and bemoan the mistakes that got them there, or they'll live in the future and destroy any chance of connecting with the present. My son was dead. I didn't cry about why he jumped or become broken by the future he'd lost. I picked up the pieces and believed in the *now*, that my son would live right *now*, and I would be there for him no matter what."

I didn't know what to say. "But your son was dead ..."

Again, she cut me off. "Yes, and yours is about to be."

That quieted me.

"The question still remains. Jaxon, are you giving up?"

"How did you do it? How is Freddy still alive?" I asked desperately, trying to get the questions in.

She smiled at me, and like earlier, looked up at the sky. "I didn't do anything."

I quirked an inquiring eyebrow. "The mothership?"

She laughed musically and said, "No, no mothership. Your friends may not know, but you do. You know exactly how it happened."

"God?" I asked uncertainly.

Holding up a finger she said, in what must have been her best alien voice, "Take me to your leader ..."

We both laughed together, and she got up from the bench. She pointed at my phone.

"Don't you have a call to make?"

I looked at the phone in my hands and came to a decision. "Yeah, I do."

I punched in a number and hit SEND. As the phone on the other end rang, I looked up and the old lady was gone.

"What the—?" I said into the empty night.

"Hello?" Sara's voice spoke from the phone. I put it to my ear as I tried to find words.

"Sara?"

"Hey, Jaxon."

"Sara, I don't want to give up."

CHAPTER 9

NO GREATER LOVE

No one has greater love than this, that he would lay down his life for another. (John 15:13, NIV)

DESPERATE BEGINNINGS

Young Destiny Hawes doesn't know what she's done wrong. *Why is this happening to me? I was a good girl.* For the last six months, all she has known is the pain and torture of the moment and the terror that leads up to each. She never knows if he will visit her that night, or perhaps the next. The uncertainty—will he bring pain, or will she sleep fitfully while she listens for him? Destiny's constant nightmare.

Lying in her small bed with her unicorn bedsheets and Care Bears blanket, she strains her small ears, listening for footsteps. She tries to focus on the glow-in-the-dark stars she's stuck to her ceiling, arranged in constellations not known to man. She gazes dreamily upon those stars and imagines herself being on a different planet, far away from the home she knows. Home for an eight-year-old is supposed to be safe, a place to escape the hurt and confusion outside. A place where a little girl wouldn't be taken advantage of. But for poor Destiny, home is a place of violation and fear.

Destiny's young strategies are exhausted. She's tried staying late at school or playing outside until the streetlights come on. Anything to keep her out of the house and away from him. Some nights, he'll pass out on the couch. Other times, he'll be locked in her mother's room with her mom, the music blaring. On those nights, safe from his attentions, she's found peace. On those nights, she can sneak to her room and climb into bed fully clothed, falling asleep immediately.

When it first started happening, she'd lain awake for hours afterwards, hurting and trying to figure what she'd done wrong. *Why is he hurting me like this?* Her young mind scrambled to think. *Maybe if I stop being bad at school? Or maybe if I make my bed when Mom tells me?* So, she started to clean more and to get better grades. She ate all her vegetables and did the dishes—anything and everything she could think of to make him stop. But nothing worked. He kept visiting her late at night, kept hurting her.

Destiny tried telling her mom on several occasions, but her mom didn't pay her any mind. Having worked all day at the local grocery store, her mom would come home and immediately start drinking. Sometimes she'd arrive home already half in the bottle. She didn't have time for her daughter's senseless words when she was drunk. And little Destiny didn't understand drunk. She only knew what her young mind told her, that she was being hurt, and her mommy should protect her.

Destiny did her best to tell her mom by throwing signals out. She cringed and hid behind her mom whenever he'd come in the room. If he spoke to her, she'd cry for what they called "no reason." She'd begun involuntarily wetting the bed, and when her mattress started to stink, her mother just flipped it over to hide the smell. One time, she'd built up her courage and told her mother that her bottom hurt. Her mother said only, "Go to the bathroom then, nasty!"

It took a lot of failed attempts to tell her mom before Destiny figured out that her mother didn't care, not at all.

She'd cried that night as the brutal truth sank in, *Mommy won't make it stop.* To an eight-year-old, that translated to *something's wrong with me.* That conclusion began its insidious growth inside her. Her subconscious used each of his abusive acts to hammer the idea home to her that she wasn't loveable, that she was a broken little girl who deserved what she was getting. That lie became her truth.

Now, lying awake in her little-girl bed and staring at the stars on her ceiling, she hears the front door open. Her tiny heart freezes as she recognizes the noises of a toolbox being set down. *Maybe he'll go to his own room tonight.* She hopes, even as she hears him ease open her bedroom door. She starts to cry as she smells the familiar stench of sweat and alcohol as he sits on her bed. Tonight will not be a night of peace, but one of pain. She clenches her eyes shut and balls her fists as she feels his hands on her skin.

"Police! Come out with your hands up!"

Lucas hears the voice, but he isn't listening.

"Lucas Mack! This is the Omaha Police Department! Exit the house with your hands in the air, or we're coming in! You have one minute!"

Lucas is concentrating on getting the needle into his arm. He's been awake now for four days, and his vision is blurry. Little trickles of blood flows like mini rivers down his forearm from where he's already missed his veins. The sting and burn make him clench his teeth as the needle finally enters his scarred vein. He pulls back the plunger and watches the blossom of blood flow into the syringe. Slowly he depresses the plunger, and the methamphetamine mixture pushes into his body. The familiar euphoria rushes into his brain, and his heart begins to fire off uncontrollably. He pulls the empty syringe from his arm and lays back on the bed, letting the drug take him away.

With the police outside, he knows it is all over now. No more drugs, no more bank robberies, no more doing what he's grown accustomed to doing. For the last twenty-six years, he's lived his life with no regard for anyone else. He is only twenty-six but feels like fifty. A life of hard living, fast women, and endless taking has worn him down physically, emotionally, psychologically, and most importantly, spiritually. His soul is drained, and he is ready for it to all be over.

Every time in the past when he shot drugs into his body, after the first initial feeling of euphoria, all the pain he'd caused in life kept crashing back down on him. Faces of the loved ones he'd hurt too many times, voices of the strangers he'd taken advantage of or robbed—these memories ran in his ears and haunted his dreams to the point that he tried to drown them out with another hit from the river of narcotics. The memories were an endless cycle, relentless in their pursuit of his mind and soul, never tiring in their tormenting.

But Lucas has long since stopped caring. Now he just goes with the flow, giving the beast inside him whatever it wants.

The cops are blaring away again on their bullhorn, and Lucas can't help but laugh out loud. The drugs are making him a little giddy. He is happy for that.

Why are the cops outside? But, of course, he already knows the answer. Charged with five bank robberies, he'd been sitting through a trial for the last two weeks. When his guilt became obvious, he'd skipped his bond and gone on the run, wanting only to cop some dope and blast his cares away. He'd been high every day in court. Even his attorney had questioned him about his sobriety. It shouldn't have shocked the court that he skipped out. They should have expected it.

His attorney has told him that if he is convicted, he would probably serve at least fifteen to twenty years in a high-security prison. That was not going to happen. No chance.

He rolls over and sits up on the bed. He picks up his dope spoon and dope sack and goes to work. He pours in about three grams of meth and a little water into the spoon. Working quickly, he pulls it up into the syringe, filling it halfway up. Next, he pulls out a small baggie of heroin and pours it into the empty spoon with a small amount of water. Once the mixture is heated and ready, he pulls it into the remaining half of the syringe. The mixture of the two drugs swirls and combines into a deadly potion. There are enough drugs in the syringe to kill an elephant. At least, he hopes so.

Outside, the cops give their last warning and commence approaching the house military-style. It doesn't matter. He'll be dead by the time they reach the back bedroom.

He sinks the needle in and laughs as he hits the vein on the first try.

"Must be destiny!" he says to himself as he depresses the plunger. The drugs gallop through his veins like stallions as the front door bursts open and flash-bang grenades explode. The last thing he sees is the ceiling in his dingy bedroom, and then his body seizes and his heart stops.

The Lucas Mack the world has come to hate is dead.

A COMMINGLING—TWENTY YEARS LATER

Destiny stepped out of the trick's Ford Focus and into the chilly morning air. The breeze brought up goose pimples on her arms and legs. Times like this she wished her job—if that's what it was—would allow her to wear more than just miniskirts and halter tops. But she knew Chi-town, her pimp, wouldn't let that happen. Whenever she'd complain, he'd tell her in his most managerial tone,

"Baby, in order to make your man some money, you gots ta show off your merchandise." If she asked again, he'd pop her in the head and tell her to shut up.

She didn't think Chi-town was a bad pimp compared to others. Sometimes he even seemed to care, like when she first met him at sixteen. She'd run away from home for the last time, and she was wandering around the downtown streets. Chi-town had been standing at a bus stop and saw her looking lost. He approached her with the look of an ally and the intent of a shark. She thought she'd found a friend, and they soon became an item. She moved in with him, and somehow, six months later, she was drug-addicted and turning her first trick.

Twelve years later, she couldn't quite pinpoint how that change occurred, but it had. Now she just lived her life and dealt with it all. As long as she was high, she could manage whatever life threw at her. Besides, she'd learned young what her lot in this world was, and she'd already come to terms with it. No need looking for a hero, not anymore.

Standing on the street corner as the car drove away, she pushed the two fifties she'd just earned into her clutch purse. She pulled out the crack stem she always kept with her, loaded a large rock, and stuck it in her teeth. She grabbed the lighter from her purse and lit the pipe, drawing a huge hit. She let the drug wash over her, then put the pipe away, pulled out a cigarette and lit up. Another morning and late night, another trick turned. Time for some sleep, she thought, as she started ambling toward home on unsteady feet.

Halfway there, she heard the sound of a car with no muffler sputtering up the street behind her. It slowed noticeably as it approached her. She turned to see a beat-up Chevy Citation—it had to be a thirty-year-old car—pulling up to her. The drivers-side, rolled-down window revealed a small, brown-skinned man behind the wheel.

He wore a big smile, and his brown eyes glowed with a certain warmth. Destiny instantly felt disarmed and suspicious.

"I'm off," she said to the man, smiling. "Sorry, honey."

"That's okay, ma'am. I'm not looking for a date. I just wanted to talk to you."

"I don't just talk," she countered. "I don't get into a car without being paid either. I'll be out here again tonight, so catch me then, baby." She started to walk away.

He put the car in gear and again came alongside her.

"Okay," he said, "I can give you twenty for allowing me to give you a ride home. That's all. We can talk on the way there. Deal?"

My apartment is only six blocks away, she thought. *If the weirdo wants to give me twenty bucks for a one-minute drive, then I'll take his money and waste his time.*

"Okay, deal," she said. walking around the car to get in. "A ride and that's all."

The first thing Destiny noticed as she got into the car was the Bible in the driver's lap. The next thing was the cross dangling from the rearview mirror and the God music playing softly on the radio. She groaned inwardly and immediately regretted getting into the car. Those Jesus freaks had tried to "turn her from her evil ways" before with their placards and picket lines. She remembered their shouts of "prostitution is evil" and "HIV is God's judgment on you!" She'd been warned to repent by these freaks who couldn't seem to see past their own righteousness to understand her pain. This guy was sure to be no different.

"My name is Lucas," the man said as he extended his hand toward her. "And you are?" She looked at his honest smile and soft eyes and found herself shaking his hand timidly.

"Destiny," she replied warily.

He let go of her hand and asked, "Where to, Destiny?"

She noticed he said her name with a certain tone, almost with nostalgia. Weird.

"The corner of 24th and St. Mary Avenue is good."

"No problem," he said, and put the car into gear. "So, Destiny, how long have you been working the streets?" The question took her by surprise.

She looked into his eyes to find no judgment there. "I don't know, over ten years. You lose count after so long."

"Yeah, I know," Lucas said.

Destiny looked at him again, expecting to see judgment or sarcasm, but found none. "What do you mean, you know?"

"I mean exactly that. I know how days blur into months, and months into years." He took his eyes off the road briefly and looked at her.

"I thought you Christians hated people like me. Why are you asking me about me?"

"Not all Christians are jerks. Some of us love you and want you to know God's love." He continued, "I know you've probably run into some of us who ... don't really care about doing anything but pointing at your sin so they don't notice theirs."

She thought exactly that.

"But there are others like me who couldn't care less how dirty your hands are. I just want to get to know you."

"You wouldn't say that if you knew who I really am," Destiny said confidently. "You'd either run scared a hundred miles in the opposite direction or start shouting me down as a dirty, filthy sinner."

"No, I wouldn't." He looked at her again.

Destiny resolved to give him a reality check.

"Last night, I had sex with five guys. Five strange men I'd never seen before and probably won't see again, ever. The night before that I had sex with a woman for fun and her husband watched. I smoke crack and snort meth. As a matter of fact, I can't wait till I get out of this car so I can take another hit off my pipe."

"Why wait?" he responded and grabbed a lighter from his middle console, handing it to her. "Go ahead, blaze up."

She looked at him incredulously. She snatched the lighter from his hand and scrambled clumsily through her purse. *I'll show him my addiction, if that's what he wants, and then he'll run back to his holy hole and never bother me again.* Putting the pipe to her lips, she flicked the lighter but got no flame. She flicked it over and over, getting no flame, then threw the thing at the windshield, cussing in frustration. She drew out her own lighter and it caught flame on the first try. The flame licked at the tip of the pipe, but she didn't pull on it.

It was at this point she realized the car was no longer moving. She continued to look at the hungry flame.

"We're here." Lucas's voice broke her trance. "What if I could show you something that could quench that thirst inside you? You'd never need that lighter again. You can leave the car now and everything will be the same. Or we can talk, just talk, and maybe you'll never need that pipe again."

Destiny let the flame die out and looked at this man she'd just met. He wasn't like the others ... what would it hurt to talk with him? Against her better judgment she put her pipe and lighter away.

"Okay. Let's talk."

He took a breath and began. "It started when I woke up in the hospital ..."

What seemed like five minutes was more like an hour. Destiny and Lucas sat in the beat-up Chevy Citation talking about life, God, and repentance. Destiny thought she'd find that Lucas would do all the talking, but he seemed to be doing more listening than anything. He told her about the cross and Jesus dying for her sins, but she couldn't seem to validate this claim of an all-loving God when her whole life seemed to contradict it.

"You say that God loves me. That he has always loved me, but you don't know that for sure, do you?" she asked.

"I do know that," Lucas replied.

"Why? Because your Bible says so?" she responded sarcastically.

"Yes."

"That's ridiculous!"

"It might seem that way, Destiny, but it's true." Lucas saw the pain brimming in her every response. "I know that it's hard to believe at first. Some of us have suffered—"

"Suffering!" she interrupted. "What do you know about that? Isn't everything forgiveness and grace to you?"

"You're not the only person who's suffered in life, Destiny, although it might feel that way. I spent eighteen years in prison, and during that time I suffered." He seemed to be drifting into the memory. "To know that the actions and decisions you made have brought incalculable torment and pain on other people brings its own prison of torment. It's no—"

"You did that to yourself!" Destiny interrupted again. "You're the one who hurt those people. You're the one who did those things to others. You were the perpetrator. I was the victim! You can't know what it's like to be on the other end of a gun. You think I asked for my stepdad to come into my room when I was a girl and violate me? You think I asked for the first guy I loved to turn me out and make me a 'ho on the streets? I never asked for this. I'm a victim, not a perpetrator. You can't know what that's like. So just sit there and shut up!" She began to cry into her hands, something she hadn't done in years.

Lucas didn't look away from her tears. He put a gentle hand on her shoulder.

"I know a victim who never asked for it and didn't deserve the pain he received. He was beaten, whipped, scorned, and cast away from his father, and then left to die upon a cross." He looked out the front window for a moment before he continued.

"You're right, Destiny. I don't know your exact pain, or even begin to know how you suffered, but I know he can. The only difference is this victim overcame his suffering so that you can overcome yours. His name is Jesus."

"Yeah, whatever, man." She wiped her eyes and face. "You don't even know me. You're only telling me these things to soothe your conscience. You don't really care."

"You're wrong," Lucas countered softly. "I'd die for you, and *he* did die for you."

Destiny grabbed her purse and opened the car door. "Thanks for the talk. Can I have my twenty bucks now or what?"

"Of course, but take this too." Lucas handed her the twenty-dollar bill peeking out of the pages of a Bible.

She grabbed the Bible and cash and stepped out of the car, slamming the door behind her. Lucas watched her go.

"Lord, give me the chance to show her your love," he prayed.

The next time he would see Destiny, he'd get his chance.

SERENDIPITY

"Lucas, are you sure these people are worth risking your life for every night?" asks Pastor Freeman.

This conversation has been going on for weeks now. Ever since Lucas decided to hit the streets and minister to the prostitutes and addicts, people have been trying to politely dissuade him from his choice. The questions have never been outright impolite but formed from a certain macabre curiosity, which frustrates Lucas even more because of their spineless nature. He's wanted to yell at them and drag them into the Scriptures, but he knows they still wouldn't get it.

He works on the streets because Jesus was on the streets. He is in the gutters because Jesus was in them. It is too dirty there for his fellow brothers, which is why they are so incredulous that he's there. He forgives them for their timidity in service to their God, and he prays every day for their spiritual awakening.

"Yes, Pastor. I wish you'd come with me one night, to see the need that's out there."

"You know I would, but I'm just so busy here with church business." The pastor makes his excuse, then exposes his hand. "Did you see the rape and murder of that prostitute last night? It was on the news this morning."

"Her name was Luwanda, and she was my friend," Lucas says.

"You knew her?" A tone somewhere between curious and incredulous tinges the pastor's voice.

"Yeah. She was eighteen. She'd been on the street for the last year." Lucas is disheartened by the glint in his pastor's eye that shows no real desire to know the girl, only to know her death in some secondhand way. He decides to try one more time to stir his friend's compassion. "I met a woman two days ago named Destiny. She's a really intelligent person. You can tell that life has really beat her down, but she still has that spark."

"Is she on drugs too?"

"Crack. But underneath all the addiction and hopelessness, I can see her reaching for a way out. I'm going to go back to her corner tonight and try to connect with her."

"Tonight?"

"She's the reason why I'm really here, Pastor. I was wondering if I could go into the funds we raised last Sunday at service. I have a feeling it's going to cost me a lot to get her attention for the night."

"Of course, son," the pastor says. "How much do you need tonight?"

"A couple hundred should do it." Lucas knows his church supports his ministry, as evidenced by their financial giving. He just wishes and prays that someday their actions would follow their cash. He doesn't know what it would take to accomplish that, but he prays it will happen soon.

He reaches out and takes the proffered bills. "Thanks."

He gets up and leaves, wondering where he'll find Destiny tonight and whether she'll be willing to talk again. Something inside him tells him that tonight he'll not only find her, but he'll reach her. The prospect energizes him.

"Dang, girl! Ain't no money out here tonight." Amber shuffles dejectedly back and forth on the corner. "Been out here for almost three hours and only made like fifty bucks. My man ain't gonna be happy."

"I hear you, girl," Destiny commiserates. "But it's only ten-thirty. We still got hours on the clock to make some more."

"Yeah, you right." Amber looks at Destiny. "You been quiet lately. What's up?"

"I met some weirdo the other day that drives around in a beat-up old Chevy. He gave me his Jesus spiel and twenty bucks for the trouble." Destiny looks out at the streets pensively.

"You talkin' 'bout Lucas?" Amber asks with a chuckle.

Destiny looks at her, surprised. "Yeah, that's him. Why? You know him?"

"He's cool," Amber says, nodding. "He's been around a few months, trying to convert us pros. I'm surprised you haven't run into him before."

"No, I haven't. He seemed like ... different. I don't know."

"Dang, girl! He got to you, didn't he?" Amber laughs.

Destiny tries to hide her trepidation. "No. Well, maybe a little bit."

"That's not a bad thing." Destiny's face shows her surprise and dismay, and Amber holds her arms out and shrugs. "We can't do this all our lives, can we? We're a little long in the tooth as it is, you know?"

"Yeah, I know. But *God?* Come on, you don't believe all that, do you?"

"Maybe," Amber admits reluctantly. "It looks like you might too."

Corner talks don't usually encompass God and life changes, so the girls are a little uncomfortable with the subjects. Destiny breaks the silence first.

"You hear about Luwanda?"

Amber shakes her head, her face dejected. "Mm-hm, sure did. They say they found her in a dumpster on Farnam Street with no clothes on and a bullet in her head. Poor girl."

"How old was she? Nineteen?"

"Eighteen. She'd only been on the streets a year. They said nobody knows nothin'."

"Of course not," Destiny says sarcastically. "Why would they? We're disposable to them. No one cares."

"You right, girl," Amber agrees. "You sho' right."

Right then a car pulls up, and the window rolls down. The john asks for service. Neither girl responds immediately, so he asks them again. Destiny looks at Amber.

"Go on, girl. I'll catch the next one."

"You sure?" Amber asks.

"Yeah, go ahead."

Amber doesn't look back as she gets into the john's car and drives away. Even with all the talk of the night, neither girl was ready right then to stop what they were doing. Even the murder of a friend wouldn't be enough. They lost at least three girls a year. It would take more than that to alter Destiny's path.

Twenty minutes later, Destiny's reverie is interrupted by the sound of a vehicle approaching. The car growls up to her and stops. It is a small truck with junk in the bed and a faulty muffler. She is reminded of another vehicle she had gotten into recently with the same problem. She bends over and looks in. The driver eyes her hungrily. Creepily.

"I got a hundred for some fun," he says, his tone eager.

A hundred? That's a lot of money. Destiny throws caution to the wind. "Let me see it."

He shows her a grimy bill. "Whaddya say?"

Destiny grabs the door handle and gets in.

"Where we goin', honey?" She grabs the hundred dollars and stuffs it in her purse.

"I got the perfect place. Don't worry." He eyes her up and down lasciviously one more time then puts the truck into gear. It rumbles its way down the street.

As the truck winds its way through the dark streets, Destiny isn't worried. She's dealt with creepy guys before. She looks around the truck and notices the plastic seat covers, and among the trash on the floor is a long length of twine and a dark bag. She looks closer. A roll of duct tape lies half-concealed by the bag. Her blood instantly freezes. Luwanda had been found tied, gagged, and stripped naked ... and dead.

She looks at the driver again, this time nervously. He glances over at her with a look of pure calculation. She tries to hide the fear in her face but fails.

"Be cool," he says, his voice ominous.

"I'm cool." Her eyes drifts to his lap. The butt of a pistol is visible under his thigh.

He sees her eyes lock on the gun, and he slams on the brakes. He reaches for her but misses as she crashes into the windshield. Dazed and confused, she scrambles to open the door. Her hand is on the door handle when his hand grasps her hair.

He pulls back hard enough to rip her head off her shoulders. She turns her head and sinks her teeth into his hand. The man howls and releases his grip, cradling his hand, and Destiny grabs the door handle and falls out of the truck. She crawls forward a few feet, tries to stand, and runs down the alley where they are stopped. A roar echoes from behind her as her attacker scrambles from the truck to come after her.

Panic bursts in her chest and clouds her mind. She calls out a name she's never used before.

"Please, God!"

Her assailant tackles her from behind with the force of an oncoming train. Destiny takes the brunt of the fall, and all the air is knocked from her lungs. Something hard strikes the back of her head, and fireworks explode behind her eyes. Her senses grow fuzzy, then dull.

The monster rolls her onto her back and begins to punch her in the face. When she does not fight back, he tears her clothes off. He rolls her back over onto her face and goes to unbuckle his pants, muttering to himself.

"Dirty slut!"

Lucas, having driven around all night looking for Destiny, is still searching for her when he comes upon a terrifying sight. The headlights of a truck in an alleyway show a woman lying prone on the ground in front of the truck with a maniac pummeling her. Lucas pulls up to the scene and leaps from his car, yelling at the man as he runs toward them, but the man ignores him. Lucas barrels toward the pair and hits the man at full speed, sending them both flying in a tangle of limbs.

The next few moments go by in a frenzied battle. Lucas rises to land a devastating punch. He straddles the man as he rains down punches. But the man bucks him off and pulls his gun, trying to bring it to bear on the small man who had interrupted his night. Lucas grabs the man's gun hand, and on their knees in the filthy alley beside the broken and bleeding woman, both men battle for the gun. Lucas launches his head at the other's face and feels a satisfying crunch as the bones of the other man's nose shatter.

They both fall over—with Lucas on top. The hard landing forces the gun from the hand holding it, and the weapon slides across the pavement and under a dumpster. Severely winded, Lucas punches the man, once, twice, three times and sees the other man's eyes go hazy. He lets his guard down for only a moment, but a moment is all his opponent needs.

The other man's knee comes up and catches him in the solar plexus, and then a crashing right hook smashes into his head. Lucas buckles and falls onto the pavement. His attacker scrambles astride him and wraps his fingers around Lucas's throat to strangle him. Lucas claws at the viselike fingers but fails to loosen them. His vision darkens, and as his fingers scrabble on the pavement from panic and lack of oxygen to his brain, somehow they find a loose brick. Desperately he grips the brick and swings it with all his remaining strength. The brick smacks into flesh and bone, and instantly the grip on his throat is gone and he can breathe again. He lies still for a few moments, regaining air. His opponent is nowhere to be seen, but abruptly the truck in the alley backs up and roars off in a spray of gravel, letting Lucas know the assailant has escaped.

He rolls onto his hands and knees and crawls toward the still unconscious woman lying naked in the street. When he reaches her, he gently rolls her onto her back. Both her eyes are swollen almost all the way shut. Her face is covered in blood. He coughs hoarsely, then almost chokes when he realizes who she is.

"Destiny!" he whispers loudly. He pulls off his coat and covers her.

He goes to pick her up but sees the pistol under the edge of the dumpster. He retrieves it in the event the monster returns. Picking up the gun, he sticks it into his waistband, then scoops up Destiny's unconscious form and carries her to his car to transport her to the nearest hospital. After he eases her into the passenger seat, he gets in and lays the pistol down. He turns the key, but the car fails to start. After a few more tries, the engine turns over and coughs to life.

Destiny, slowly regaining consciousness, feels herself being carried and set into a vehicle seat. She hears the man get into the car, but she can't see well because of the pain and swelling in her eyes and face. She realizes she is naked now, barely covered by a jacket. As the engine struggles to start but fails, panic overcomes her. She knows this man is going to kill her, just like he killed Luwanda.

Her hazy vision clears as the engine catches, and her eyes lock on a gun lying on the seat next to her. She snatches it up immediately and barely aims before the gun roars in her hands, deafening her in the small space. One, two, three, four, five, six, *click, click, click.* Empty.

She looks around her.

How did I get here?

Straining to see through her battered, bloody eyes and the smoke from the gun, she focuses on the form next to her and on the face wheezing through bloodstained lips. Her body goes limp as she recognizes Lucas in the driver's seat. His shirt is blood-soaked.

"Lucas!" she screams, almost maniacally. "*Lucas!*"

"It's okay." Blood runs from the corner of his mouth as he speaks.

She leans toward him, gun still in hand.

"I'm—I—" She tries to speak to the dying man but can't find the words.

"I know," he says softly.

She looks into his eyes. The utter peace in his gaze flows into her. His hand grasps hers lightly. She grips it back.

"Please forgive me!" Her voice is desperate.

"I already have." He struggles for breath, and a ghostly smile flickers across his face.

Must be destiny.

He releases her hand. "You have to go. Get away from here before—"

"No!" she pleads. "I can't!"

"Please, go ... it's okay."

The look in his eyes gives her the strength to open the door, and Destiny crawls from the car and stumbles from the scene, sobbing.

The last thing Lucas sees before he dies is the cross dangling from his rearview mirror. The last word on his lips is the name of his God.

CHAPTER 10

YE THAT EATETH, SHALL NOT SMEARETH

"It's a scorcher out here!" Lucinda Torres exclaimed in awe to Amelia, her lovely escort and sister-in-Christ, as the two made their way across the park toward the church picnic. To be exact, Lucinda—or Ms. Lucy to the church folk—was rolling across the grass and Amelia was diligently pushing her wheelchair.

"Darn tootin' it's a scorcher," Amelia agreed. "I can already feel the sweat beading on my face. One of these days, Ms. Lucy, I'mma leave you at home so I can take a break from this servitude."

"You'll do no such thing!" Lucinda admonished good-naturedly. "Look at these skinny arms! I'd be house ridden. I need to be out here amongst my people."

"Yeah, yeah." Amelia laughed. The friendly banter between the two was a common refrain, something both women took joy in. At eighty-two, Lucinda was confined to her wheelchair because of pain from decades of arthritis. But she never showed her suffering because she was always so joyful, which is what had attracted Amelia. Like Lucinda, Amelia was single, never married, with no children and no desire to start a conventional family. At forty-two, Amelia's childbearing window was nearly closed, but that suited her just fine. She had all the family she needed at Open Arms Worship Center, the church where the two women served. The pair had become the church's unofficial beloved mascots. The diminutive Black woman pushing the even tinier Latina around town was the embodiment of Christian love and friendship and a source of pride for everyone at Open Arms.

Now as the two rolled along the grassy turf toward the gathering of brothers and sisters, they could hear the sounds of laughter and joy. Christian praise music was being pumped through a sound system, and several large grills promised a variety of fragrant fare. The smells and sounds of happy fellowship enveloped them as they drew near.

A few congregants saw the approaching duo and rushed to greet them. Even though they could see Amelia working hard to push her charge across the grassy lawn, they knew better than to offer help. Amelia took her service to her friend as seriously as Secret Service agents did toward the President. She would not be deterred or relieved from her welcome duty.

The fellow party goers welcomed the two women with warm greetings and hugs, then walked with them the final few feet toward the picnic tables. One sister in the group chattered away amiably.

"It's so good to have you ladies with us! Pastor told us to make sure we saved you two seats together and we surely did, right here at the head of the picnic table. Wait, is there a 'head' at a picnic table?" Without waiting she charged on. "Anyway, you're right here. And anything you need, all you need to do is shout."

"Thank you, Elitcia," Lucinda responded as Amelia rolled her to her spot and locked the wheels into place, then banged on the brakes to ensure they were secure. Amelia wanted to make sure they didn't have another Market Street episode.

They'd been rolling along on Market Street. During a brief stop, Amelia failed to lock the brakes in place, which led to a most interesting and quite thrilling chase down Market Street. It ended when the hill started to elevate in grade, decreasing Lucinda's speed enough for the trailing, flailing Amelia to catch up and corral the chair. Lucinda could still feel the bracing wind gusting across her wizened cheeks. Of all the ways to go home—now, *that* would have been glorious. Poor Amelia had never forgiven herself, even though by the time she'd caught the runaway chair the occupant had been screaming, not in terror but in pure unbounded joy. The two ladies looked at each other, saw the reflected terror and exhilaration, and burst into equal parts laughter and tears. When they calmed down, Lucinda had looked at the apologetic Amelia, who was terrified she'd be dismissed on the spot.

"One more time?"

That comment led to more gales of laughter and permanently bound them in sisterhood.

Amelia took her seat at the picnic table next to Lucinda as their escorts went to welcome more new arrivals. She poured two glasses of lemonade and handed one to Lucinda, who was smiling and waving her greetings.

"Here, Ms. Lucy." She set the cup in front of the smiling senior. "It's nearly ninety degrees. You need to drink something."

"What are you, my doctor? I need to be told when to drink something?" Lucinda loved jibing her friend even as she took a sip. "I wonder what kind of grub they have at this fiesta."

"Well, if Mrs. Jenkins can't tell us, then no one can." Amelia nodded toward a rotund woman walking their way with a plate piled high with goodies.

Lucinda looked toward the lovely lady and her smile faltered for a second. By God, she loved everyone at Open Arms with the heart of Christ, but Mrs. Jenkins could rapidly deplete even her stockpile of grace. Whenever Mrs. Jenkins arrived it was with a flurry of social tidbits and a whirlwind of rumors and gossip. Lucinda, never one to be rude, was always at her wits' end trying to redirect the conversation toward something edifying. It was a job she did not want to partake of on this sultry day. She sighed loudly, and Amelia snickered.

Mrs. Jenkins approached at top speed and eyed the empty spot on the bench next to Lucinda's chair. The two women locked eyes, and Mrs. Jenkins took it as assent and welcome and bustled over merrily. Lucinda braced herself for the coming conversation by saying a quick prayer for patience and grace, then looked at her new tablemate with genuine warmth.

"Mrs. Jenkins," Lucinda said in greeting. "Nice to see you here."

Mrs. Jenkins squeezed herself onto the bench seat.

"Good day to you, Ms. Lucy!" She set her plate of food down and leaned over to place a hand on Lucinda's. "Always wonderful to see you out and about." She nodded toward Amelia. "And it is lovely to see you, Amelia. The sight of you two ladies of the Lord always sets my day aright."

"Of course, Mrs. Jenkins," Amelia replied with a smile of sisterly love.

Lucinda squeezed the hand gripping hers. "So, Mrs. Jenkins, tell us, what's the food situation here? I may not look it, but I'm ready to eat my weight in grilled cuisine."

Mrs. Jenkins sat back. "Well, let's see ..." She eyed her plate and pointed with a plump forefinger. "I'm having a grilled burger, potato salad and ... hm, I think this is some sort of fruit salad. But the special thing about this plate"— here she leaned in for effect—"is the secret sauce."

"Secret sauce?" Lucinda asked.

Mrs. Jenkins pointed to the sauce generously applied to her burger.

"Brother Todd makes a mayo that is to die for. I don't know what he puts into it, but I swear, Ms. Lucy, it's ambrosial."

"Well, I'm sold," Lucinda said. She looked at Amelia who was already rising from her spot on the bench.

"A burger and ...?" Amelia asked.

"The works, sister!" Lucinda admonished. "If my plate is any less cluttered than Mrs. Jenkins's here, then you'll need to make a second trip."

Amelia laughed, joined by Mrs. Jenkins who said, "And don't forget the secret sauce! That's the key!"

"Yeah, yeah, it's the key." Amelia shook her head as she left the two women at the table.

Lucinda looked over from her chair at Mrs. Jenkins, who was digging into the grilled burger. She was wearing a black and white summer dress with a large black hat. In the sweltering air, the sweat shone on her face.

"Girl, I don't know how you wear that black dress in this heat!" Lucinda mused aloud. "I'd shrivel up like a raisin faster than I don't know what!"

Mrs. Jenkins took the hat off her head and fanned herself. "You sho' right, Ms. Lucy. Probably not my best fashion choice!"

Just then a couple approached their table. It was the Grays, Frank and Tammie. The young couple looked happy as they came closer, faces alight with joy. Their marriage had been on the rocks, and they'd only recently rededicated. It was beautiful to see them together again, and Lucinda beamed her satisfaction at them.

"Frank, Tammie!" she spoke loudly. "How nice to see you two! Come here and love on Ms. Lucy!"

"Ms. Lucy!" the couple said together as they hugged the tiny woman in her chair.

"I can't tell you how happy I am right now," Lucinda said while grasping a hand of each spouse before letting them go.

"We wanted to thank you. Ms. Lucy," Frank began. "Your prayers and kind words helped us through and ... we have news." He nodded toward his wife, who looked near to exploding with the news.

"We're pregnant!" Tammie Gray blurted.

"How wonderful!" Lucinda crowed while pulling them close for more hugs. "The Lord blesses us even in the valleys!"

"Yes, he does," Frank agreed while looking with love upon his wife. "Well, we just wanted to share the news. We're off to spread our joy."

The couple ambled off, exuding love in all directions. Lucinda's heart was filled up as she watched them leave, until Mrs. Jenkins spoke.

"I wonder if Brother Jim's heard that particular news," Mrs. Jenkins breathed softly.

"Excuse me?" Lucinda responded, taken aback.

"Everyone knows the reason the Grays split up was because Brother Jim was … well, let's just say the fox in the hen house," Mrs. Jenkins said, a faintly lewd gleam in her eyes.

Lucinda was flabbergasted. "We—I don't know how that's any of our business."

"Oh, come on, old girl," Mrs. Jenkins continued. "Everyone knows it! Frank spends weeks at a time on the road for business and leaves poor Tammie on her own. It's no surprise she wandered. I surely don't blame her. I heard it told that Frank caught them in the act, and the police had to be called."

Lucinda knew most of these facts were wrong but held her tongue. She knew the other woman was fishing for more information at the same time she delivered these obvious lies. This was the exact verbal badgering she had hoped to avoid with Mrs. Jenkins.

She closed her eyes and said a quick prayer for peace. When she opened her eyes, she saw Mrs. Jenkins take a large bite from her burger, and she sighed in relief. Maybe the food would distract the busybody from her gossipy prey … but no. No sooner had the large bite gone down than the woman continued her line of attack.

"I mean, they're twenty-three! Should they even be married so soon? Young people today need more time to figure themselves out," she stated with a self-righteous harrumph.

Lucinda was about to reply when she noticed Mrs. Jenkins had a new addition to her makeup. Slowly sliding downward from the corner of her mouth was a large globule of Brother Todd's secret sauce. The snail of sticky goodness was leaving a greasy slime trail in its wake. Mrs. Jenkins, oblivious to her facial plight, kept up the talk.

"Come, Ms. Lucy, I know you know some juicy details." She leaned in closely and the condiment paused its journey, resting in the shade of a convenient crease.

Lucinda pulled her eyes from the transient sauce to look Mrs. Jenkins squarely in the eye.

"I don't even know where to start with that question, Mrs. Jenkins, but you have—"

Her attempt to alert her sister-in-Christ to the need for a napkin while diverting the conversation was foiled by Mrs. Jenkins, who would not be denied.

"No buts, Ms. Lucy." Mrs. Jenkins leaned back in her chair and began speaking once again. The wayward dollop began its descent in a leisurely fashion, its hostess none the wiser.

"I say, once a cheater always a cheater, and Frank would be smart if he kept his eyes open because ..." The gossip continued her rant, equally oblivious to her audience's fascination not with her dialogue but with the secret sauce's path of defiant dilatory divergence.

My God! Lucinda thought to herself. How can she not feel that? The woman kept up her harangue, and Lucinda couldn't pull her eyes from the gelatinous mass. *Surely she notices me staring at it? Maybe if I shift my eyes back and forth?* So, Lucinda tried eyeing the glob and then flicking back up to Mrs. Jenkins's face, but that failed to do anything but boost the woman's confidence.

"I know," Mrs. Jenkins gushed, thinking the flickering eyes were a visual cue of shock. "I was surprised too! I mean when ..." And she dove right back into her soliloquy.

Lucinda groaned in frustration, both with the conversation's content and because the absconded ingredient had taken another break in facial perambulation, stopping less than an inch from the bottom edge of the woman's chin.

This was torture. *Fall off already*! Lucinda tried to psychically bully the schmutz into moving again, but to no avail. Just when she was about to blurt out some rude declaration to Mrs. Jenkins, Amelia returned to the table. *Thank God,* Lucinda thought, as Amelia set her plates in front of her. *Surely Amelia will know what to do.*

"All right, Ms. Lucy." Amelia interrupted the current conversation with some good-natured ribbing. "If you eat all this then you'll have to wheel yourself back over there. I nearly had to wrestle Sister Mary for the last serving of Brother Todd's secret sauce. Boy, is that stuff popular!"

Sure enough, there it was. Lucinda looked at her plate and there, in an innocent mound, was a small portion of the wandering wayfarer topping. She pulled her eyes from her plate and looked at Amelia imploringly, and then over to Mrs. Jenkins. The sauce was still there, taunting her.

"What?" Amelia caught the look and turned in the direction of Mrs, Jenkins. Her eyes immediately locked onto the condiment and her mouth quirked slightly.

Mrs. Jenkins must have thought to herself that Sister Amelia was not aware of the juicy gossip of the day, and considered it her duty to remedy the situation, because she began again.

"So, Amelia, let me tell you what you missed. Wait, first let me take another bite of this burger."

Dear Jesus, *no*, Lucinda silently begged. Amelia saw the frustration in her friend's eyes and the sauce on her sister's chin. She did not interfere, but instead regarded both Lucinda and Mrs. Jenkins with a look of barely contained humor.

To Lucinda's absolute horror, when Mrs. Jenkins finished her second bite there, in the almost exact same place of the first globule, but on the opposite side of her mouth, was its twin.

Amelia coughed into her hand to hide her snort of laughter, but still pointedly disregarded her friend's dismay. Lucinda watched as the first deposit waited patiently while the second one began to mosey its way south.

To Lucinda, Mrs. Jenkins now seemed like some condiment-draped vampire as she began to espouse even more lurid and most definitely false details. How the woman could talk and not feel the hitchhikers on her face was beyond Lucinda's understanding. All that was needed was some carnival theme music to add to the surrealness of the moment. That, and possibly an announcer to announce rail position, like they did at the Kentucky Derby last year.

The second hanger-on pulled adjacent to the first and then, in synchronized movement—which did not surprise Lucinda in the least—they began to lay down twin contrails of greasy goodness on their way to Mrs. Jenkins's chin's edge, where they paused again in silent obstinance.

Just fall already! Lucinda gripped her chair's armrests, and this time Amelia let her chuckle escape.

Mrs. Jenkins paused in her tale with round eyes and a Fu Manchu moustache of still more secret sauce.

"Yes. I know, it's funny, but—"

She was interrupted by the reappearance of Frank Gray. Mrs. Jenkins had the decency to look chagrined and immediately quieted.

"Ms. Lucy, one more thing," Frank began, but then looked at the other two women and apologized.

"I'm sorry for interrupting, ladies, but—"

He looked toward Mrs. Jenkins. "Oh, Mrs. Jenkins, you have something on your face."

Mrs. Jenkins looked confused as she touched the right side of her chin. Her fingers came away sticky. "Oh!" She immediately dabbed that side, cleaning up the mess.

"The other side too," Frank gently pointed out.

"Why, thank you." Mrs. Jenkins quickly cleaned up the other side while glaring at the other two women. Her face turned a bright shell pink.

Frank saw it and spoke quickly to cover her embarrassment. "Well, Ms. Lucy, I just wanted to say that what you did meant a lot. No, now, don't deny it! Going over to the doctor's office with us was above and beyond. We'd been struggling to have this baby, and without your encouragement and presence we might've given up."

"I just follow the Lord's prompting," Lucinda said modestly.

"Yes, well, I just needed to say thanks again." Frank dove in for a generous hug and then departed. The ladies watched him go.

"That's a blessed marriage," Amelia said, with a huge grin.

"Yes, yes, it is," Lucinda agreed. When the two women looked back at the table, Mrs. Jenkins was no longer there. She must have made a quick retreat during the distraction. Lucinda exhaled loudly.

"What'd I miss while I was gone?" Amelia asked innocently.

Lucinda looked over at her with narrow eyes.

"Don't you even start! I ought to unlock these brakes and make you chase me down Market Street again!"

"You better not!"

Both women burst out laughing. Every time the laughter slowed, one or the other of them would snort and get it all started again.

After several minutes of joy and tear-stained cheeks, Lucinda wiped her face and casually picked up her plate.

Using her plastic spoon, she scooped the secret sauce from her plate and let it fall into the grass. She watched as it nearly splattered an itinerant ant, who stopped to investigate.

"I think I'll pass on the sauce," she said.

And both women burst into laughter again.

CHAPTER 11

BREATHE

Here there is no Greek or Jew, circumcised or uncircumcised, barbarian or Scythian, slave or free, but Christ is all, and is in all. (Colossians 3:11, NIV)

LEE

How can you express the innate sense of 'other' that you have lived with your whole life, whether a person of color or not? How can a person who has never lived under the constant pressure of cultural assimilation understand the blessing they've been given? I live with the understanding that any misstep you make will condemn your whole race. And to add more pressure where the burden is great, there is a government agency ready to usher you back into oblivion, or to physically put you back in your place with a quick beating or a frivolous harassment. These are things every Black person in America must deal with on a regular basis. We struggle under this burden of racial injustice. It's not fair to have to live under such scrutiny and fear.

I'm a Christian, and there is a Scripture in Colossians that talks about the unity we have in Christ, that no differences are made in the kingdom of God. We are all equal in God's eyes. When I first read that verse, my spirit jumped after that truth. To finally be equal in all things is a dream of every Black American. I struggle to hold on to that truth in a country that is expected to live up to that principle yet falls so colossally short.

At my home in Broken Arrow, Oklahoma, I stand at my kitchen counter watching the evening news. My wife Brenda stands at my side as the newscasters explain why an officer charged with the killing of an unarmed Black man has been freed and the charges she faced have been dropped. My hands clench on the counter as the anger inside me boils. I can't listen to any more of the legalese used to excuse the actions of the officer involved. To me, as it is for many Black Americans, it is just an excuse to allow another execution. This latest use of deadly force by an officer against an unarmed Black person is just one in a string of recent murders, and only adds another brick in the wall of systemic racism every Black person faces. This time, the brick was a bullet in the back. Last time, it was a knee on the neck. Next time, it could be a choke hold. Who knows? The bricks keep adding up, and with the growing height of the wall, there is growing fear and anger in my soul.

"It's okay, baby." My wife comes behind me and wraps me in her arms, laying her head on my back. I say nothing. I know she can feel the tension building in me. "We need to pray for all of those involved. The Lord will take care of them."

God bless my wife. She's the best thing that's ever happened to me. She completes me in a way I never thought anyone could. We're just so different that when I fell for her it was out of nowhere and completely soul-rending. God brought us together, and I have no doubt that he is using each of us to heal the wounds of the other.

My wife Brenda is White, raised in the suburbs of Broken Arrow. Her upbringing was so far from mine socially that at times we struggle to empathize with each other. Our marriage separated her from some of her family, and I am constantly aware of the sacrifice she lives with every day. Not to say that my family was any more eager to add her to the familial roll call. The standoffishness was only broken by a word from my grandmother, Big Mama. She took one look at Brenda and saw the soul of my wife, the absolute goodness there, and immediately ordered the family to accept her. From then on, Brenda has become an integral part of our family. There is no racial lens on her eyes. She sees only people whom she loves with the power of Christ, and I love her for it.

For all our love, my wife and I have never truly had an honest conversation about race. It's always been something we silently overcame by the strength of love, a giant we slew in our devotion to each other. With everything going on in the country, the racial tension has grown nationwide, and has slowly crept into our household. She feels it, as do I, which is why she clings so tightly to my back right now, as if her physical proximity can close the gap between us. I breathe deeply and wish that was the case. But it's not, and we both know it.

"Why won't they stop killing us?" I ask quietly. The question shatters the solace of our moment of peace.

"I don't know." I can hear the pain in my wife's voice. "I don't know, Lee."

I turn around and face her, needing to tell her what I've been thinking. I can't let the wall being built outside on the streets of our city enter our household any longer. I will tear it down with honesty and lead my wife by baring my soul to her.

"I'm going to go protest tomorrow," I tell her, and the fear for me enters her eyes. "I need to have my voice heard with the others out there making a stand."

"Why, my love? We just need to stay prayerful and wait on God to move," she implores, and I feel the attraction of the simplicity of prayer and its effectiveness.

"I know God moves, Brenda. I also know God is moved by our action. I can't keep sitting by watching the TV as

Black people are killed and do nothing. It's killing me too."

"You don't think I see it?" She pulls away from me and takes a step back. "I know you, Lee. You're my husband. And I fight for you and this country every night in prayer."

"It's not enough," I say plainly, and my wife is taken aback.

"Since when is prayer not enough?"

"When it's time to link that prayer with action. It isn't enough to simply have faith if that faith isn't producing works."

"Are you saying my faith is empty?" She's angry now. I'm lousing this up.

"Not at all, my queen," I say, in an effort to placate her. "I'm sure there were times in the sixties where well-intentioned people urged the civil rights marchers to stay home. They saw their loved ones being beaten and arrested, and they begged those in the fight to pray, to leave it in God's hands. But they'd been praying and leaving all the work up to God for a hundred years, and the time had come for action."

"And you're saying that's what's happening now?" She seems mollified by my explanation, but then she never stays angry for long. "You're saying you need to be a part of this? I just didn't think you felt the same as the protesters. I mean, you're married to a White lady."

She says this with the faintest flick of her eyebrows, and I smirk in return.

"These protests aren't against White people, my love. They are against the social injustices every Black American faces. They're not a referendum on White citizenry, but against police brutality. Our marriage," I said, and pulled her back against me, "is a blessing from God. It happened despite the hurdles we faced. You know that. Racism is real, and you felt it the moment we came together. We've just never talked about it in the open."

"I thought our victory was enough. Why? Why do we have to keep fighting?"

"Welcome to the struggle, my wife. Your privilege has been revoked." I try to joke, but my comedy only stirs her anger.

"*What* privilege?" Her anger returns in full, and she breaks free of my grasp. She stalks to one end of the kitchen, then turns and stalks right back. "I never chose to see color! I never accepted any privilege! When my family tried to pressure me, I never bent. Not for one second."

"I know," I agree, but then I speak my heart. "That's the privilege right there. As a White person, you get the privilege to choose how you interact racially with the world around you. You get to choose if you will see color or if you won't. If you want to close your eyes to race, you can choose to do that, and the only time you'll feel repercussions from that decision is if you choose to link up with the other side. If you hadn't married me, you could've continued to live in your racial neutrality." I can see she's listening.

"Black people?" I continue. "Black people have no choice on how we'll interact racially with the world around us. Our racial standing is in no doubt. Each of us has to fight for every inch we make toward equality, knowing that if any misstep occurs, we'll tumble down the ladder we've been climbing."

"I never thought about it that way." My wife's naïveté is lifting as her paradigm shifts. "I always thought of my neutrality as a badge of honor."

"I know, and it is in some ways," I agree. "The sad part is not that you feel that way, but that we live in a society that directs your thinking in that way. We live in a country where racial ambivalence in the White population is seen as a positive attribute. It's one of the obstacles that Black Americans must overcome. We, and I mean all of us, don't need neutrality or ambivalence to change the world we live in. We need people to pick sides. Will we stand for justice for all? Or justice for some?"

"Have you always felt this way?" Brenda asks with concern. "Like I was failing you?"

"Never!" I speak with sincerity. "Never have *you* failed me, but I've always felt this way about our country. Do you know what my first experience was like with the police?"

"No." She steps close to me, and I wrap her up again. "Will you tell me?" I can see the openness in her face and her desire to hear me. It opens something inside me.

"I was seven," I begin. "And my mother took me and my brothers to the store with her. Randall was ten, and Konrad was eleven. We were all belted in and having a great time. Road trips were a favorite for us boys because we played road games like padiddle. You remember that game? Anyway, we were maybe ten minutes into the ride when a police cruiser got behind our minivan. Mom shouted at us to be still, but what did we know about the danger we were in? I was seven, my brothers slightly older. To us, the police were our friends. We continued playing until our mom shouted us down. Her voice seemed to shock us into silence, and then, the cruiser hit its lights. My mom pulled over to the curb and all hell broke loose." I breathe deeply.

"Two more cruisers arrive, and the officers all jump out of their cars with weapons drawn. My mom starts to cry, and my brothers are straining to see behind us. I'm frozen in my seat as the cops approach the van. They are screaming at my mom, saying if she moves, they will shoot her. Now my brothers are both crying, and my mom is still as a rock with both hands on the wheel. The cops yank open the driver's door and slam my mom to the concrete. She's hollering, begging them not to hurt us. Then they pull open the van doors and my brothers disappear in a blink. The cop that sees me has compassion and gently pulls me from my car seat. He sets me down and tells me to lie on the ground, but the pavement is hot! I start crying, hollering for my mama, and Mom starts to resist from her prone position on the ground.

"She's trying to come to me. The police Taser her and cuff her before they throw her in the back of a cruiser. My brothers are both cuffed and made to sit on the curb. We're all crying."

I don't realize I'm crying even now, until a tear splashes on my chin. Brenda pulls me tight.

"I'm so sorry," she whispers.

"About a half hour goes by and the police realize the van they were actually looking for had an out-of-state plate. Same number, but different state." I snort. "You know what they did?"

"Let you go?"

"As if," I scoff. "They took my mom to jail for resisting arrest and had Big Mama come to the scene to pick the rest of us up. It was only after Mom had spent hours in custody that they finally released her. That day, and the fear it instilled in me, lives on to this day. It's reinforced every time I'm followed in a store, or any time I'm racially profiled and pulled over, or any time I'm looked at askew when I walk into a store with my White wife. And that fear has slowly morphed into anger. Most Black people have similar experiences and similar fear that they deal with."

"I never knew," my wife says with passion.

"I understand. It's one of the struggles Black Americans live with. How do you communicate this sense of fear and hopelessness to a large portion of the population who happen to be in control? Whenever you speak on it, it is seen as 'playing the race card.' There's a portion of the media out there whose job it is to confuse the issues and politicize every killing of an unarmed Black person. They'll bring up the dead person's past or say they were resisting. Or use the protests to cloud the issue of a flat-out murder. Then when the police get off, they've already built in the ambivalence we fall back on." I pause. I can tell Brenda is thinking deeply.

"When I watch these videos of people being killed," my wife starts, "I am always ticked off by that. Why does it matter what he's done in the past? Why should it matter if she resisted? I get so appalled when the media suggests that the appropriate sentence for these victims is summary execution. When we have kids, I don't want to worry about our sons being executed because they panicked and ran from the cops. I don't want a call from the coroner's officer to tell us our daughter is there because she tried to pass a counterfeit twenty-dollar-bill."

"That's exactly it, baby," I agree passionately. "I understand George Floyd's fear of the police cruiser. Who knows what abuse he was reliving at that moment? Yet the police saw that fear as belligerence and punished him for it. Unfortunately for everyone involved, their punishment led to Floyd's death, but think about how many Black people face that without death. The police are out of control, my love. I have to stand with the people in the streets."

"Even if it means you get arrested or hurt?" I can feel her fear returning.

"Yes."

A sudden resolve fills my wife's eyes, and a palpable wave of love emanates from her spirit.

"Then I'm coming too."

I pull her into a hug and breathe into her neck as I speak to her. "I never doubted it."

STEVE

Officer Steve Kocevar, ten-year veteran of the Broken Arrow Police Department, gingerly removes his shirt, avoiding the deep bruise on his chest, and places the shirt in his locker. With only ten minutes until his shift starts, he dresses for this day's war. He hates thinking of the next eight-hour shift as a battle to be survived, but unfortunately that is what it has become.

Last night had been particularly violent when the police and protesters clashed. Rubber bullets and broken bricks had been exchanged, each side taking heavy casualties requiring retreat. Thankfully no one in the crowd suffered more than minor injuries, and no police officers were seriously injured. Injured, but not seriously, as his bruised ribs could attest.

Officer Kocevar pulls the Ace bandage from his locker and begins to wrap his aching chest. He had been one of the unlucky officers to take a flying brick to his ribcage. Although the pain is intense, nothing is broken, and for that he feels thankful. Last night—or was it this morning— he had slipped into bed silently without waking his wife. Tina had always been a worrier, and telling her that he was injured would have been a mistake. She would baby him and ask him to call in sick, which, of course, he can't do. Five hours later, he sits on the bench in the precinct, ministering to his own bruises and hoping he can find someone who has some extra ibuprofen before his shift starts. *Please Lord, if not ibuprofen, at least bless me with some Tylenol.* Something to dull the deep ache in his side.

He finishes the last wrap and fastens it tightly as he thinks about the coming eight hours.

The outrage and despair flowing from the crowds on the streets are palpable. At first, he'd looked at this assignment as purely crowd control and tried not to get caught up in the politics of it. As time passed, that attempt at unbiased shielding was shattered. He stood on the front lines locked arm-in-arm with his brothers in blue and couldn't help but see the looks of pain and hear the voices of the crowd.

The cries for justice and equality only gained more traction in his heart as the guys next to him fired bean bags and rubber bullets into the protestors. As the tear gas canisters flew, his heart broke more and more for those he was supposed to protect. *Is this serving?* he asked himself repeatedly over the course of the night. The red, swollen eyes, streaming gas-burned tears, seemed to accuse and condemn as he looked into the faces of those he'd committed his life to helping. *I don't feel like the hero of this story*, he'd thought, even while taking that brick to his ribs. Especially then.

Church service on Sunday helped some. He'd left feeling rejuvenated by the pastor's message of love and hope and was ready to serve his community with a renewed sense of passion. Then his shift had begun, and in his heart of hearts he agreed with the protestors. The officer charged was a rookie who had acted out of fear and killed an innocent man. Everyone on the force knew she'd been in the wrong, but woe to the man or woman who did not stand by her side. The thin blue line was real, and any officer who broke ranks would be vilified and blacklisted by their coworkers until they left the force.

How can one man change a culture? It was an excuse that no longer brought him any solace. Now he only feels conviction as he batters people on a nightly basis. Thirty-three days of nightly vigilance is crushing Steve Kocevar's desire to enter the fray once more.

His thoughts are interrupted as he finishes dressing when his partner, Jamal Freeman, enters the locker room. For the past three years, he and Jamal had served their community side by side and gained a brotherly love that only comes from facing the fire with another and having that person come through for you. The young Black officer is ten years his junior, but that energy serves as a catalyst in their friendship. After ten years on the force, a person needs someone by their side to bring the fervor and passion back to the job. Officer Jamal definitely brings that.

"Hey, partner!" Jamal greets his friend as he goes to his locker to dress for the day. "Why you look so blue? Heh, get it, blue?"

Steve can't help but smile at the terrible joke. "I'm good, buddy. Just a little sore from last night."

His partner looks over at him while dressing.

"Yeah, that was a nasty hit you took. Friggin' protestors lobbing bricks! What do they think this is? A free-for-all?" Freeman says with disgust. "No matter, I'm pretty sure we busted the head of the thrower ... or at least one of his friends." The officer chuckles.

Steve doesn't join in on the laughter as he holsters his gun quietly and shuts his locker. Jamal notices his silence and takes it as a rebuke.

"What, man, you feelin' a certain way about last night?" the younger officer asks.

"I don't know, Jamal," Steve says stoically, trying not to let the confusion he feels enter his voice. "I look at those crowds every night and wonder if what they're fighting for isn't legitimate."

"What!"

"You heard me." Resolve is growing in Officer Kocevar. "Don't you think that we only reinforce the concept of police brutality with every swing of the baton? You know I'm no bleeding heart, but the movement out there in the streets we're called to serve is being led by those we're called to protect. Doesn't that give you pause?"

"Movement?" Jamal asks with derision.

"Yeah, movement."

"Black Lives Matter and all that? I got news for you, Steve, all lives matter. Not just Black lives." Officer Freeman pauses, then continues. "And what? Don't our lives matter? Or do we get abused for no reason every night?"

"Of course, our lives matter. Don't be ridiculous!" Steve snaps back. "That isn't what Black Lives Matter means, that Black lives matter more or White lives matter less or that blue lives matter not at all. It means only that the Black lives being taken matter. You have to admit that the videos of people, Black people, dying by our hands have exploded. I can't believe I have to explain this to you of all people."

Jamal looks at his partner with surprise.

"Why, because I'm Black? Because I'm Black, I should side with the people lobbing rocks at us? Nah, I have my own mind, partner. I choose to think for myself. And just to be clear, it only appears that more Blacks have been getting killed by police because of all the videos. Statistically speaking, police shootings haven't gone up dramatically."

Officer Kocevar laughs while shaking his head. "Oh, so Blacks have been getting killed at this rate by police for years, is that your argument? It's only because of the videos that we're seeing it with our own eyes. That doesn't help our cause, it helps theirs! Why do we have to shoot someone for resisting, or choke someone to subdue them?"

"Because that's how we're trained!" Freeman cracks back. "Shoot until the threat is neutralized. Meet force with overwhelming force. Protect and serve. This is the duty!"

"No, partner." Steve disagrees softly. "I think that is the problem."

Jamal steps up in Steve's face and pokes a finger in his chest. "What's up, partner? You goin' soft on me? Do I have to worry about you not having my back? Tell me now, so I know if I have to request a new partner. One that won't wilt under pressure."

Steve lays a hand on Jamal's shoulder while leaning his face close to his partner's.

"I've known you for three years. I will never leave your back exposed." Passion fills his voice. "We're brothers, and I pray that God will bring us through this fight in one piece. I also pray to God that this is the right fight and that we're on the right side."

"We are." Jamal shrugs the hand from his shoulder. "Now let's go. We've burned enough time with your whining. It's time to boot up."

Officer Kocevar watches as his partner leaves the locker room with all the self-righteousness of the young. He wishes he felt so certain of his duty. That surety had fled moments ago. Taking a deep breath, he follows his friend out the door and onto the front lines.

LEE

The crowd outside our car pulses with energy. After so many weeks of protesting, one would expect some of the fervor to leave the gathering, but with each day's passing, the passion continues to build. It's exciting to be a part of something so enormous. To feel like you are making a difference in the struggle for justice is fulfilling. This is the third weekend for Brenda and me, out on the streets protesting. Every day we march feels like we're getting closer to change. Yesterday, the police agreed to make substantial adjustments and are instituting a community review board to make citizens part of the review process for police shootings. The mayor was seen marching lockstep with protestors, and even the Vice President tweeted his support. It was a start, but we want more, and that's what today's rally is about. The community organizers are pushing for a refiling of charges for the death of Jacob Williams, as well as an internal review of the prosecutor's office that dropped the charges. The plan for today is to march on City Hall and protest outside the District Attorney's Office. Our voices will be heard.

The protests last night were violent again, and the national media is focusing on these agitators' actions. The protest organizers tried to get a handle on the violence, but with outside organizations coming in, it was near impossible to do that. Too many other groups held different agendas for the rally to have a single, unified message. All we could do was hold our rallies during the daytime, then retreat home and lift in prayer those left on the streets. The nightly clashes were disappointing and always left the daytime filled with anxious officers and protestors unsure of what the next moment would bring. Would rocks start flying, or tear gas be launched, and the peace of the rally devolve into violence? We prayed that wasn't the case.

After our pre-rally prayer that we say every time we come down, we exit our car into the filled streets. I look over at my beautiful wife as she comes around the car wearing her Black Lives Matter shirt with her blonde ponytail bobbing underneath a hat that reads *Say Her Name*. Brenda never does anything halfway. Before hitting the streets with me, she spent hours on the computer learning about the movements out here and choosing two organizations to champion. I was never more proud of her than when she came out of our bedroom dressed in the garments of her conscience. I'm a lucky man.

"It's beautiful, isn't it?" she asks me as she comes alongside me, talking about the sea of faces in the crowd. I smile and agree as I clutch her hand.

"Yes, it is." The crowd is filled with people of all races, ages, and genders. Elderly White men stand next to young Black women who are linked arm and arm with Hispanic fathers. It's the epitome of the forces needed to make changes in our society, a gathering of communal strength and love from across the spectrum of our community. Every day as we come out and march in these crowds, the fear and anger that has built in me has eased, and a slow confidence in progress has been growing in its place. It does my soul good to be here, to experience this unity.

"Black Lives Matter! Black Lives Matter! Black Lives Matter!" the community of protestors shout together as the march commences. The crowd begins to move down the streets as one, echoing the chants for justice. Brenda and I join the throng, and holding hands, add our voices to the many. This is what it feels like to truly be a difference-maker.

Along the streets in small groups are counter-protestors. They hold signs that say, "All Lives Matter" or "We Stand with the Police" and wave them at us while shouting obscenities and wearing *Make America Great Again* hats. Marching past these groups used to aggravate me, but now I only feel compassion. I wish I could sit across from them and tell them my story while I hear theirs. I can't help but feel their angry faces are contorted in ignorance, not villainy. I don't understand why justice for Blacks seems to offend them so much.

The heat of the afternoon soon beats down on our group as we move through downtown Broken Arrow on our way to City Hall. The cries from the crowd change to "Say Her Name!" as we twist and turn through the streets as one. People hang from open windows to add their voices to the cacophony, some in support but some not, and they wave American flags from their rooftops. The atmosphere of the rally begins to ratchet up with every group of counter-protestors we encounter, with each group antagonizing the other.

"Lee," Brenda says to my left. She can feel it too.

"It's okay, my love," I comfort her. "We're almost there." Not once during the daytime has a rally devolved into violence, so even though I feel the energy shifting, I try to dispel my disquiet. For the next few blocks, I tell myself everything is fine and nothing is going to happen. It's not until we turn the final block and see what is there to greet us that I fully understand what's in store for us.

Lined up in military-style fatigues and body armor, holding shields and batons and shotguns are rank after rank of police. Their helmets and visors obscure their faces, and the anonymity lends the force a certain aura of unknown violence. Their body language reeks of pent-up aggression, and at the sight of the crowd, they ease forward like hounds held steady only by some unseen leash. Not in all our days of marching have we seen a daytime display like this. All of our rallies up until this point have been peaceful, and the surprise of this antagonism flies through the gathered protestors. Surprise morphs into indignation, which quickly turns into growing anger. The protestors see the escalation and react.

I feel the sweep of emotion and momentum as we flow toward City Hall, now only a few hundred paces away. Chants of "Ja-cob Will-iams, Ja-cob Will-iams!" roars from hundreds, perhaps thousands, of throats in unison. I hear my wife's voice blend in with mine as we chant. The air of the protests is charged. A group of police break off from the cordon in an attempt to split our group.

The police attempt to form a wedge and batter the crowd into separating, but they are a pebble in a wave of justice and are swept back into their previous formation. The looks on their faces at such a rebuttal are blanked by the visors blocking them, but the raised batons promise retribution for any further action.

The line of protestors spreads out and I find myself on the front line about five feet from the armored officers. To my left is an elderly White man, the same one I saw at the beginning of the march. He looks at me and gives me a nod while chanting. I look to my right and Brenda is there. She grabs my hand, and we continue our calls for justice. The police line in front of us is ominous, and I can't help but recall the fear of a seven-year-old as I confront them.

"What do we want?" someone on a bullhorn calls out.

"Justice!" the crowd answers.

"When do we want it?"

"Now!" we answer.

These calls continue for an hour while the energy ramps up. Behind the officers, on the top steps of the courthouse, a woman in a pantsuit steps out with her own bullhorn.

It's the District Attorney. Her perfectly coiffed hair seems out of place with the sweaty visages of the protestors. She holds up her hands for quiet and the crowd roars loudly one more time.

"Ja-cob Will-iams!" And then we get quiet.

Laura Ashcroft, District Attorney in Broken Arrow, collects herself and speaks to the crowd.

"We thank you for your dedication to see justice served. The city stands behind you. We do! We hear your voice and are working toward change in the future." She takes a breath. "As far as Mr. Williams goes, we have already adjudicated that situation and stand by that decision. Please accept that. We're sorry for any feeling—"

"What?" someone hollers from the crowd. It's the elderly man next to me. His outrage is written across his face. "That's it? You're sorry? We want justice!"

The crowd roars its approval as the District Attorney flees back into the safety of City Hall. The elderly man next to me steps forward and is met by two police officers, one Black, one White, linked arm-in-arm. The clarity of the moment strikes me as they bar the man's way. The elderly man is still shouting at the retreating lawyer and the crowd bays its discord. All I feel in that moment is utter disappointment. Our voices are not being heard. What will it take to get justice?

The next few moments happen in a blur. The elderly man steps forward and the Black officer reacts immediately. He hits the elderly man with a shove from his baton that sends the senior tumbling backward head over heels. I see the man falling, but I can't react quickly enough, and I hear the impact of the man's head contacting the pavement. He does not cry out or move to get up, and I kneel quickly at his side. Brenda is at his other side while the two officers loom above us. Blood pools beneath the unconscious man's head and leaks from his ears, indicating serious injury. My wife and I lock eyes in our shared fear for the man's life. For me, that fear quickly coalesces and lights up in righteous anger. Brenda sees the change but can't get to me fast enough to stop my next actions.

I stand, and inside me is all the fear from twenty years ago. I see my own mother laid out on the pavement being Tasered and arrested. I hear my older brothers hollering for our mama. I feel the heat of the concrete scalding my young skin and searing into me the understanding that I am helpless. All of this emotion quickly surges forward and overwhelms my reason and faith, leaving me filled with white-hot rage.

I look at the two officers, and they can see it. The officer who assaulted the bleeding man narrows his eyes, and I can hear the second officer shout, "No! Wait!" But I explode into action, incoherent, deaf to conciliation. I close the gap between myself and the first officer, and as he swings his baton, I duck and shoulder-blast him in a linebacker hit. He is lifted off his feet and thrown back into the cordon of police offers as I bellow in rage. I turn to the second officer quickly, expecting an attack, but in his eyes I see only compassion, not hate. I'm pulled from behind by my wife, whose hand is wrapped tight in my shirt like I'm a bucking horse and she's a rodeo rider. My fury reaches a new level as I see the first cop regain his feet, and the whole line takes a step forward.

I can't hear Brenda screaming my name. I can't feel the shock in the crowd at the sudden violence. I don't even stop to consider the consequences of what it would mean to take on a hundred armored officers by myself. I only know I won't be scared any longer. I won't be broken by the knee on my neck that is institutional racism. I will fight back. I step forward to meet my fate with all the force of my will and body. The police are only too eager to oblige.

The first officer plunges forward and before he hits me, the second officer pushes him back violently. Their visors have been lifted in the scuffle, and I see the look of betrayal on the first one's face as he looks at the other. I can't hear what's being said, but the second officer is shouting at him with his hands out in front of him. With his back to me, I notice the officer's holstered handgun is less than one step away. I could grab it and ...

Just then the officer faces me. His eyes track mine, and he sees what I'm thinking. Our eyes connect and all the sound comes rushing back. The fervor of the crowd, the fury of the police, my wife's screams for her husband sounding like my mom's cries from the pavement, all of it crashes in on me as I look at this officer. He speaks to me.

"I know," he says. "I know."

It only registers now that I'm crying. Tears rush down my cheeks as my rage and fear mingle in this debilitating concoction of pure emotion. My chest pumps like a bellows, my fists clench at my sides and my jaw is clenched so tightly my teeth may shatter. The White officer in front of me with his earnest eyes and his amazing courage steps forward and puts a hand on my heaving chest. My first instinct is to break it off, but with that contact something in me snaps, and I feel a corresponding break in the officer.

My wife clings to my back as I break down into sobs. The officer keeps saying, "I know. I know," over and over, and I feel his free hand clasp the back of my neck. Our heads come together, flesh against helmet, and all the tension of the moment abruptly unfurls and drains away. With blurry eyes I look to see tears on the officer's cheeks, and he takes his hand off my chest, offering it to me. I grasp it with both of mine, and in some unspoken understanding we take a knee.

The crowd has fallen completely silent. The police have backed away, and a medic is now looking over the prone form behind us. Like a wave of serenity, a spirit of magnificent awe has coalesced here among us, two broken men and one loving wife, and the crowd collapses to one knee in unity. The sight of two tear-streaked combatants humbled by grace is too much even for the officers lined up for battle. They quickly follow suit and then it is just us again, in that moment.

My wife weeps behind me, still latched on tightly to my shirt.

The officer asks, "Can we pray?"

I nod humbly and he begins.

"Dear Lord ..." With every word he speaks, the presence of God solidifies. His prayer is spoken with such clarity and focus that his voice carries over the heads of the people, so much so that those in the back of the crowd can hear it. The words reverberate through me fully, and I feel something seeded long ago pulled up by its roots. In its place is planted a new seed, one with a new harvest to come. The officer ends his heartfelt prayer with, "In Jesus's mighty name, amen."

To our amazement, the entire gathering of police and protesters echo the "Amen." I look up into this officer's eyes. His nametag says *Kocevar*, and I know I've met a friend for life.

I finally hear the words my wife has been repeating for the last few minutes.

"Breathe, baby, breathe," she whispers.

And just like that, I can. I don't know what the future will hold. All I know is that I can ... breathe.

CHAPTER 12

BUTTERFLY TRILOGY, PART 3: THE FALLS

The fiery globe in the sky beamed down relentlessly upon the desert floor. Everywhere it touched, life was tested. Only the most resilient of creatures or plants survived the desert's inferno.

Two creatures walked through the sands in relative peace. They traveled under the shade of the only cloud in the sky, and their every step was in cooling sands instead of searing agony. As long as they stayed under the cloud's protection, they found their desert trek tolerable. However, staying underneath the cloud required them to follow the cloud's trajectory and direction. As of right now, the man, the butterfly riding on his left ear, and the cloud seemed to be heading the same way—toward the distant mountains.

"Well," Web said, "the mountains look to be only a couple days from us."

Lily flitted from his ear and flew a few feet ahead, then returned to his ear.

Music floated on the air and resounded in Web's spirit. An excitement filled his chest as Lily spoke to him.

"Yes," he agreed. "I can't wait either. Rest ... finally."

They continued their way through the wasteland with new urgency. For the last few days, the desert to their left had been changing shape, forming into craggy bluffs.

The unwelcoming sight promised more strife than the hot sands of the familiar dunes. Lucky for them, Web thought, the mountains ahead would be a place of solace for him and Lily.

Hours passed with the mountains, now colored in shades of green, growing closer and closer. Lily took flight from Web's ear and flew into the air. She flew in gleeful patterns, enjoying the wind on her wings. She glided through figure eights, loopty loops, and other joyous patterns until she felt the familiar heat of the sun blaze upon her wings. She immediately returned to Web's ear and chimed in his ear ... bewilderment.

Web had stopped in the sand too. His eyes were on the sky and on the cloud that had taken a new course. Instead of heading toward the mountains and tranquility, the cloud headed in the direction of the ominous bluffs. The blazing sun danced across the sands again, and Web's feet grew hotter as he contemplated the change. This was obviously a crossroads in their journey.

Should they continue the last leg toward the mountain without the cloud, or should they follow the cloud's shade into what looked like guaranteed hardship?

Lily chimed again—*uncertainty*.

"I know." Web agreed. "We could make it to the mountains on our own."

Lily played a tune reminding him of their travels without the cloud and the dangers.

"So ..." Web considered. "We follow the cloud?"

Lily chimed once again—*uncertainty*.

"Okay." Resolve entered Web's voice. "We follow the cloud."

The bluffs loomed larger and larger with every hour that passed. Their intimidating heights were tolerable only because of the cloud's reassuring presence overhead. If the bluffs' presence had been coupled with the sun's rays, things would have been much more difficult.

The mountains were growing smaller and smaller in the background, and with that, the finality of their decision weighed on Web. Had they made the right choice? Should they have continued toward the mountains? He knew Lily would have followed him wherever he had chosen. He hoped that he had not led them to their doom. The bluffs growing closer and closer did nothing to assuage his conscience. As a matter of fact, they seemed to mock his ridiculous choice to approach.

As they walked, Lily sensed his discomfort and yearned to dispel his fears. She, too, felt the same way. Should she have tried to change their course? She could have. He would have listened to her if she'd tried. But under the cloud's presence, even in the shadow of the bluffs, there was a sense of ... destiny.

Taking flight from Web's ear, she flew in a figure eight and alighted softly on his nose.

As usual, Web stifled a sneeze and smiled brightly. Lily played a tune—*assurance*.

"Thank you," Web said gratefully. "As long as we are together we can make it."

Lily chimed—*agreement*.

"Well," Web said with renewed strength. "We're here."

They stood at the foot of the desert bluffs. The rocky walls and shallow ledges stood uninvitingly before them. The cloud's presence continued on and left the pair in the shadow of the bluff walls.

"Oh, great!" Web blurted out angrily. "Where is it going?"

Lily chimed her confusion along with him.

The cloud rose over the bluffs and stopped, the first time it had done so. When it came to a rest just past the ridgeline, it seemed to settle in with finality.

Was this where the cloud had been leading them? Web

stared at the landscape, confused. To a rocky bluff? No. There had to be more, something at the top of the bluff.

A dry wind began to blow, bringing with it the dusty heat of the desert behind them. Lily would not be able to fly the sheer heights in this blustery wind. She'd have to ride along with Web. They'd have to ascend together, hand over hand, a daunting task. Then Lily, in what sounded like a newfound resilience, chimed confident tones to Web, and her tune bolstered him.

"We climb," he said as they came to the craggy wall of the bluff. "Hold tight."

The climb was even more difficult than it looked. Handholds that seemed solid disintegrated under pressure and left the pair dangling precariously as Web struggled to regain his balance. Footholds that felt sure broke apart as he put his weight on them, and again the pair would scramble for safety. Every muscle in Web's body screamed as they ascended.

By the time they reached the midway point, Web's fingers were scraped raw, his knees were bruised, and his nerves were in shock. Overcoming a particularly nasty protrusion in the cliff face, they were surprised to see a deep shady cave in the bluff's wall. Gratefully Web climbed over the lip and Lily took flight into the cave as he stumbled in behind her. Web collapsed in a heap on the cave floor. Lily landed on her perch.

They lay there as Web breathed heavily, his muscles slowly relaxing. The wind outside the cave howled and blew dust into the cave. The thought of having to continue up the bluff in those conditions was not a welcome idea for the exhausted pair.

After a prolonged rest, Web sat up. He knew that if they continued to lie there, they would never want to get up and go on. He rose to his feet and walked to the cave's mouth. The wind had settled into a steady howl. Looking down at the desert floor, he found it didn't look as far away as he'd thought it might be. Then he looked up and immediately wished he hadn't. The wall seemed to stretch to the horizon. Flexing his stiff, bloody fingers, he put one hand on the cliff face and continued upward.

"Here we go," he said with determined resignation.

The second portion of the climb was no easier. Several times they found themselves either dangling in mid-air or having to move laterally to avoid horizontal protrusions. With every hour of the climb, with every heart-pounding slip, Web's strength sapped. Several times, Lily was blown about dangerously before landing on him again, migrating around his body with every new obstacle he had to climb. By the time they neared the top, they were both nearly tapped out.

Focused as he was on the climb, Web didn't realize they'd reached the end of their journey until Lily chimed in his ear. He looked up and saw that only ten feet remained to climb. Lily took flight, and when she reached the top, a violent wind blew her out of sight.

"Lily!" He scrabbled the last few feet in seconds and hoisted himself over the cliff's edge in a panic. He stood in his disheveled state, knees bruised and scratched, fingers a bloody mess, sweat pouring from his sun-darkened skin, and his chest heaving with exertion.

Then he smiled. The view before him was beyond anything he could have imagined.

Lily returned to him, flying circles around his head in a blur of color and chiming amusement. Web found himself chuckling along with her at the absurdity of what they were seeing. Nothing in their unbelievable existence had prepared them for this.

The cloud above had descended to hover about fifty feet off the ground, its cottony texture continuously folding and rolling in upon itself. It seemed so close to the ground that Web thought if he reached out, he could touch it. Lily could fly up to it, yet it seemed to emanate an untouchable quality that induced a kind of reverence. The sight of the cloud was breathtaking, and below the cloud was an even more amazing and impossible sight.

Hanging in the air, almost pouring out of the cloud, but not, was a waterfall. Its waters appeared out of nowhere and fell to the ground beneath the falls. When they hit the ground, they entered the dry earth in a soft spray of water and earth. There was no pond, no brook, no puddling of water whatsoever. The water simply disappeared into the ground in a steady flow, sending up a mist at the bottom, a watery veil filled with shifting rainbow hues.

"Wow!" Web said lamely. It was the only word he could think of to describe what he saw.

Lily alighted on his ear and chimed her agreement. Web walked closer to the falls and stood a few feet from it, feeling the damp mist on his skin. He'd expected the apparition to fade and vanish as he grew close, but it did not. The feel of water on his skin only bolstered its existence. He walked around the sides of the falls, not sure what to expect. To his surprise there was nothing behind it but more desert. The view from the side was jarringly impossible. How could this be?

Once again at the front of the falls, or the back—he wasn't sure which was which—he knelt at the base. Lily chimed apprehension as Web reached forward with cupped hands and plunged them into the falls. Water filled his hands in a rush, and he pulled them out and drank.

He felt a familiar rush of energy as the liquid hit his stomach. Quickly he refilled his hands and continued to drink. As he did, his energy returned, his hands were healed, and the bruises on his knees were no more. These were familiar waters ... the oasis?

He stood up as he thought about this. Lily flitted from his ear and landed on his hand. She'd seen his reaction to the water, seen his hands healed and his energy return to him. Landing on his finger, gently she lowered her tiny head and sipped water off his finger, then took flight and flew dizzy patterns through the air.

Web laughed as she flew through the misty air, playing a tune of jubilation.

"Woooo!" Web hollered his exhilaration with her. She landed on his nose with wings atwitch. A tune of anticipation touched Web's spirit.

"I don't know," he said in response. "What do we do now?" Before Web could even think further, Lily took flight from his nose in a blur. She flew with impossible speed straight into the falls and disappeared.

"Lily!"

Web jumped up and sprinted to the other side of the falls, expecting to see Lily burst through the other side, but she wasn't there. He looked around quickly then hurried back around. She had not reemerged from the waterfall. She was simply ... gone.

As Web stood in utter confusion, contemplating what had just happened, there was a blur behind the falls. Then as he watched, a form took shape. It was completely without detail. It was the shape of a person standing on the other side ... or the inside? The figure was short with long hair, and it seemed to be bouncing on its feet.

Then it stopped bouncing and reached forward. Out of the falls stretched a dainty arm from the elbow down. The small hand was held out in an inviting gesture. Realization dawned.

"Lily?" Web asked in bewilderment.

Music issued from the falls in response.

Web reached forward and grabbed the hand around the wrist. The hand immediately latched on and tried to yank him into the waterfall. He snatched his hand back and yelped. Music sounding a lot like laughter floated out of the waterfall, and Web couldn't help but laugh along a little sheepishly.

"You little minx!" he said, rubbing his wrist and smiling. The hand stretched out of the falls again, but this time he was ready when the hand snagged him. He answered by tugging playfully back. Joyful music filled the air and Web laughed too as he finally stepped into and through the falls.

On the other side, Lily pulled Web through the water and into her waiting arms. Web fell against her, dripping wet, laughing loudly. He looked down into her cherubic face. Her eyes, their colors ever-changing, crinkled with joy as they drank in the sight of each other.

They stood ankle-deep in waters beside a gentle waterfall that a fed a small stream. Web looked around and noticed on this side was a small cliff surrounded by trees. The music of songbirds filled the air. They were back in some part of the Oasis. Lily's home.

"We're home," Lily said, seeming to read his thoughts.

"But how?" Web asked puzzled.

"Silly man," Lily replied with a giggle. "Always questioning. Never thinking. The cloud brought us here."

"Oh. But how—" Web began before Lily silenced him with a soft kiss.

"No more questions. No more desert," she said as she led him out of the stream.

They walked for a short while, and the soft grass under their feet absorbed the sound of their movement. Web drank in the sight of Lily as they walked, watching the movement of her small frame and flowing hair. He was stunned by her beauty more and more with every second that he saw her. He barely noticed his surroundings.

The sun hung gently in the sky, illuminating the forest. The forest creatures walked about in absolute peace. An abundance of butterflies fluttered to and fro, making beautiful music. At one point Lily was covered with at least fifty of them crawling over her flawless skin. She laughed and talked to them as they landed and took flight back into the trees. Flowers of every conceivable color and variety were in full bloom, adding their aromas to the scene. This was a place of fairy tales, Web thought.

They came to the largest tree Web had ever seen.

Huge white flowers and green leaves filled the branches. There were large hollows, rope ladders, rope bridges and small human-like structures all throughout the giant tree. Looking up, Web saw that the tree never ended its ascension, and its breadth was astonishing. As he watched, a butterfly landed in the upper branches and then a shimmer surrounded it. Out of this shimmer stepped a small human form, a woman, who turned and waved down to them. Lily waved back, and Web grabbed her hand and waved too.

They were laughing as Lily shouted up into the branches.

"Hello!" She dragged Web closer to the tree, but he stopped. Stubborn. Nervous.

"What is this place?"

Lily knew Web needed to hear her next words in his spirit, so she pulled him close and whispered in his ear.

"Home."

She watched his face as peace smoothed his fears. Web felt himself relaxing as the words sank in. They'd made it. They'd actually made it. He looked into Lily's smiling face and returned her smile.

The burning sands faded from his memory as Web's journey finally came to an end.

"Home," he repeated to Lily. "Home."

CHAPTER 13

EPILOGUE: TAKING THE FIELD

I look upon my King as he sits upon his throne. The throne room is a vast chamber made of solid gold brick, the walls encrusted with every jewel a mind could envision. The entire space is empty—no bench seating, no place for a weary body to find rest. Which is fitting since there are no weary bodies here. Light pours in from far above us, giving the impression the ceiling is made of glass. All sound in this ethereal bastion, crystalline in clarity, carries perfectly to the ear no matter the distance. A word spoken at the chamber door is heard unhindered by the listener near the throne.

And what a throne it is, made of platinum and diamonds and set on an elevated dais of large, interlocked rubies. It shimmers in the effervescent light. The footstool before it is the only imperfection in the room, made of the broken and battered armor of the Death Knight who was vanquished by my King in millennia past. The rusted metal scrapes against itself, as if crushed in the hands of a small child and cast aside recklessly to land here at my King's feet. There it serves its purpose, a visible declaration that even death is subservient to the Lord of Hosts.

The throne on which my King sits does not face the large throne room. Rather, the throne faces outward toward a massive window opening, empty of all glass. The window gives my King an unobstructed view of what lies outside and below his kingdom. He has invited me numerous times before to look out upon that view, but I know what I would see.

Both awe-full and incomprehensible in its vastness, I would see man's complete existence laid before me, outside the constraints of mortal time. Everywhere I looked, I would see battles simultaneously raging. From the left side, beginning in the Garden, my view would move to the gathering host of armies in the deserts beyond that, then to a struggle of "modern" armies fighting futilely to the right, and in the center, an empty cross dominating a broken army of darkness. To focus on any one point, all I would have to do is merely will it, and that area would come into perfect clarity. I could watch an ancient force enslave freedom to its political whim, and with a minute twitch of the eye see that enslavement crushed by a lone priest nailing papers to a rickety door.

I've looked upon this field before, but I've not done so again. The mortal mind was not built for such sights, such computations. Man's channels of reason and logic were not created outside of time but in it. I will leave its translation and coordination to my King, for when he looks upon the expanse, I see comprehension and confidence that calms my fear. I trust my King, for he created it all. Looking upon my King now as he sits on his throne with his feet perched on the rusty footstool, I am filled with ease.

Once I did not feel such peace. The first time I saw him, shining like the noonday sun, my legs turned to jelly, and I fell at once to my knees. My tongue had begun to speak on its own, confessing every imperfection of my soul. It took quite a while for the last words of my mortal disobedience to slip past my lips. When it was finished, I expected this great King to lay me low in his perfect justice. Instead, I'd been lifted to my feet and pulled into an embrace that obliterated every blemish. I don't know how much time passed, for time has no meaning here. But when the embrace was broken, I found myself dressed in royal colors, and my King ushered me to a place of honor amongst the Witnesses. A vast crowd of past rebels welcomed me into their midst, and we took our place watching our King's exploits in the realm below us. It was a great joy and exaltation to stand among them and take part in the order of the kingdom. I'd never felt so free and without restraint, and I knew without a doubt that this King would never end, for this place knows no endings.

My King came for me this morning. How I knew it was morning I do not know, but my King has asked me to sit at his side and witness, which is how I came to be here in his throne room. I look upon his kingly visage and am awestruck once more.

His youthful features are fixed in a look of contemplation. The dusky complexion defies any racial bounds and is completely smooth and vibrant. His mouth is built for joy, a mouth that always looks on the verge of smiles and laughter, inviting you along for the ride. When a smile does break through, you feel encompassed by the dimples that bracket his face. His nose is a centerpiece that draws all your attention to the eyes above.

Oh, and the eyes of my King ... they sit below a gentle brow but are of a color to both break your spirit and envelop you in their protection. The iris's color is a molten black suffused with magenta veins. Imagine looking into the core of an active volcano with its burning ferocity, and you come close to the perpetually incendiary quality of the King's gaze. His eyes have been described as coals, but that mundane encapsulation pales in comparison to the reality. Crowning and enhancing all of this is a magnificent mane of snow-white hair. The unbounded waves flow from his head down across his shoulders, and their perfect embrace gives the whole of his appearance a forceful, yet ageless, wisdom. He is both a Prince and a King, Youth and Age, together in perfect balance.

The doors to the throne room are thrust open and a mighty being boldly approaches the throne. The being looks to be a man, only much larger, and from his back great wings stretch forth. He wears scorched armor and a great sword scabbarded at his side. His martial stride and bearing give no doubt that this is a being mighty in battle, a warrior to be feared. The look on his face defies his body's posture and appearance, for it gives off a certain love and relief. He looks like a general at the end of a bloody campaign, ready to be relieved of command.

I witness as he finally reaches the throne, salutes with a fist to his chest, and awaits the King's attention. My King slowly looks over, and when his eyes land upon the warrior, his face glows with his smile. The warrior immediately falls to his knees.

"My Lord," he says humbly. "I come to give you a final report."

The King moves from his throne to his champion's side, raising him to his feet and brushing the battered armor with his mighty hands.

"No need to kneel any longer, Michael."

Everywhere the King's hands brush, the armor is instantly made new and shining once again.

"You have served us well. In no other kingdom could a more worthy general be found. Come, my son, come. Let us hear your report so that we may know your heart's content."

The King ushers the newly invigorated general to stand by the window, then takes his seat upon the throne. With a look, he invites me to join them. Filled with trepidation, I approach the two and look upon the field now spread below us. Everywhere the eye lands, battle is engaged, and above a mighty wind gusts to and fro. In every place the wind touches, beleaguered troops are renewed and begin to fight more fiercely than before. The sheer magnitude of what is transpiring forces me to look away and back toward my King and his general. The two look upon the battlefield with an understanding I am incapable of, so I merely stand and witness.

"Report, General," the King commands gently.

The general stands taller and begins.

"Yes, Lord." He points to a place of vibrant sands. "In the Agape Desert, things go well for General Web. He has broken through the enemy's pathetic attempt to overrun his position, and even now he leads idyllic infantry to victory."

I look to where he points, and immediately brought into focus is a battered man with some creature perched on his ear. They lead an angelic force through deep sand littered with the broken bodies of their sulfuric enemy.

"In the East, General Kocevar and Lee have the Hate Knight in retreat after a close battle." He points to another field of carnage where three people, two men and a woman, kneel together in a huddle, surrounded by both friendly and enemy forces regrouping for another engagement. "It was a near disaster, but my King's plans for those three have proven fruitful."

"As we knew they would," the King says with a knowing smile.

"Yes. Yes, of course." The general returns the smile and continues his report. I can only marvel at this leisurely conversation during such peril.

"You'll find this quite enjoyable. Young Sergeant Javon Samuels has broken the Fear Knight with only a quill. It seems that fear is something the young, like Javon, are not nearly so susceptible to. As our enemy has now learned."

The two share a laugh, and I get the sense this briefing is not for the King's benefit but for the battered general. He begins again, and with every description of victory and defeat his strength returns, and the King looks more pleased. At that moment, the King looks at me and gives me a sly wink. I'm shaken to my core as I realize the revelation I've been having was placed there by the soft breeze on my neck.

The King is once more listening intently to his general's words.

"Lieutenants Lucy and Amelia have rallied Corporal Jenkins and have the Proud Knight at their mercy." The general does laugh this time and continues. "We can't rely on the Proud Knight's defeat, for he is a worthy foe who rebounds from defeat regularly. I'd suggest sending reinforcements."

"Noted," my King says with feeling. "Reinforcement is near."

"The Doubt Knight may have broken General Jordan." The general sighs sadly. "The great Pastor is in disarray, but surprisingly a new general, one Jake Evans, has grasped the standard, rallied the troops, and leads a new resistance against what was surely defeat. The angelic host was quite surprised by this development."

The King is not surprised but looks kindly upon his servant. "Unlikely victories are what we do, Michael. I would think you'd be past the surprise."

"Yes," the general agrees. "But this one was ... obstinate in his refusal. Now, he serves. It's amazing." The general pauses for a moment, then continues. "Colonel Francis Neagley holds firm in his faith at his daughter's bedside, refuting the Knight of Lies. Never has there been such a resilient soldier as Francis, and he wins more to your cause every day."

"Tell us of our Special Forces Commander," the King instructs.

"My Lord, this commander is special." The general's countenance takes on a stoic appearance. "General Hawes has crushed the Shame Knight."

When I hear this name, my spirit lurches inside me.

"Destiny has trod upon its desiccated remains and

leads a holy contingent against Addiction's fortress. The lost and forgotten all flock to her banner, and the Enemy trembles at their advance. A more tenacious army has never been fielded, and your glory mounts with their every victory."

I turn from the general to find my King's eyes upon me once more. I am filled with satisfaction and gratitude as he looks once again upon the servant before him and speaks.

"Thank you, Michael," he says gently. "Your service to us will always be held dear." He places a hand on the general's shoulder. "Now go. Remove your armor, hang up your sword, and take your place at the head of our host. Your King will take the field soon, and all will be complete."

The general looks so satisfied I fear he may collapse. "Thank you, my Lord."

He strides from the room in seconds, leaving me and my King alone. A span passes before my King speaks into the silence and breaks my heart with his simple words.

"So, Lucas Mack. Witness to me," he asks. "What have you seen?"

"Your victory is near, my Lord." I stammer on about what I have heard, but stutter to a complete stop as I realize I'm avoiding what I really want to say. My King looks at me with that half-smile, and his burning eyes sear away any pretense. I speak.

"She thrives."

The half-smile blooms full. "Yes, she does. It's fantastic, isn't it?" The pure joy in his voice is childlike, yet full of depth.

"It is, my King," I agree, as we look upon each other. His obvious satisfaction begs me to continue. "I ... I never thought ... I mean, I hoped—"

"Of course."

"But ... to know that my Destiny—" I stop at how presumptuous that sounds. "I mean *your* Destiny."

"It's all right, Lucas, we did that together, and it is good."
He encourages me with his kind words, and we share in a
celestial shout of utter joy. Then he comes down from his
throne, and I dance in jubilation with my King. Only when
we stop, when my cheeks are covered in tears of joy and I
look at my King's wonderful face, do I understand. This has
all been part of his plan, and everything that has happened
has come together at this very moment.

I recall my King's final words to the general, and I
shudder in anticipation as we look at each other. "You're
taking the field."

He responds with a fierce, knowing smile and a single
nod. "It is time. Get my armor, Lucas."

I rush to the side of the throne where his shining armor
is racked, a carapace of pure light. I've seen this work of
artistry before, but now as I handle the beautiful work, my
fascination is renewed. I lift the breastplate, which seems
to be made of constellations and galaxies contained inside
clear crystal. The captured magnificence swirls and shifts
majestically as I carry the featherweight armor to my
King. As he straps on the breastplate, the luminescence
gains brightness, and every star and nebula pulses with
mesmerizing energy. With a shake of my head, I clear my
vision and return to the rack to retrieve the vambraces and
greaves. I pick them up, barely noticing how they shimmer
from one color to the next—blood red, ultramarine, gold,
and emerald green. They flash as I hand the vambraces to
my King to attach to his forearms while I kneel and secure
the greaves to his shins. Once on his body, the shifting
colors intensify, and my Lord's presence solidifies into
awe-inspired terror. It is only with a word and a gesture
from him that I am not struck completely dumb.

"My sword, Lucas." His hand on my shoulder sends
me fleeing to obey his command. I find the sword leaning
against his throne, and it is only with great reluctance and
care that I dare to lay hands upon it. The hilt is unblemished

ivory, and the length of the great broadsword is battle-charred metal. The appearance of the blade is that of an ageless dormant star awaiting the spark of ignition. I transport it to my King's waiting hand, hoping it doesn't burst into flame and immolate me with its slightest touch.

"Thank you, Lucas!" My King laughs and takes mighty swings with his sword. He looks at me and says conspiratorially, "You think this is something?" He takes another huge cut of air with the blade. "Just wait." And he booms another earsplitting laugh. I find myself laughing too, despite my fear of this mighty King.

The huge doors to the throne room burst open again, and a soul-rending music fills the space. Along with the music, a great white stallion comes thundering into the room. The giant steed stands at least thirty hands, his skin rippling with ferocious muscle. I quiver at his approach.

He skids to a halt on unshod hooves and dances, tossing his mane with an ecstatic whinny. My King laughs at the display.

"Nimbus! " he calls. "What an entrance, my friend!" The horse whinnies in response, and my King launches himself into the air and lands catlike on his back. "Well, Lucas? One more ride?"

He gives me a hand onto the horse's back behind him. My King snaps the reins, and we trot out of the throne room in a gust of wind. Outside, the angelic host sing their worship, and the song infects me too. We all sing, and my King smiles as we fly through the golden streets.

In moments, we come to a blazing stop before two enormous gates. The pearlescent gateway is barred, and I look at my King for guidance.

"This is as far as you and I may go together," my King informs me as he hands me down from Nimbus's back. "The rest we will do on our own. You, Lucas, must stand Witness."

I stare up in awe. "Of course, my King."

My King raises his sword and gives a mighty shout, and a terrific howling begins. Only as the gale-force wind hits me do I realize it is the source of the howling. The wind hits my King and coalesces into a tornadic funnel that finds its home in the raised sword in my King's right hand. The fierce wind is sucked into the blade and the entire sword bursts into flame, throwing sparks in all directions.

My King points the burning weapon at the gates, and at his signal, the gates slowly open. The great host moves behind him, and with his holy armor gleaming, his snowy hair shining, his gaze burning, and his mighty sword alight, my King takes the field.

AFTERWORD

This book and its stories are still growing, still finding new characters and plots to give them life. I could have continued to write and fill pages, but I chose these stories because they best represent my most fruitful realizations so far along my walk. Any more stories, and I felt like we might have gotten lost along the way.

I'm praying what you have read has caused you to stop and have conversations with others in your life that you love and care for. Conversations that you may have felt were perhaps ... "unholy." Let me explain that.

I was raised by two amazing women and grew up around a church family led by an awesome pastor. My mother is a woman of high moral standards (and after coming to Christ is now a Sunday School teacher). My aunt, who is more like a big sister, is a missionary along with her husband. My pastor, who has always believed in God's plan for me, is a giant in the Christian community, coming from generations of tent-reviving faith blazers. Which, taking all this into consideration, would make one believe that the spiritual atmosphere where I was raised was idyllic.

I mean, Mom's a Sunday School teacher, my aunt a missionary! My pastor is one of my biggest allies! This seems a golden situation for spiritual growth, right? In almost all areas you'd be right. Among these pillars of

Christian faith, I stand now and thrive, thanks in part to their faith in me. I thank God daily for them. I am blessed.

There was one specific area where I found I struggled in the midst of these backers, and that was transparency. How could I open up to them about my issues? Faith, doubt, fear, lust, anger? They'd left them all behind years ago, right? I felt … unholy or unworthy, when I'd struggle with these things, and I found I couldn't speak on them without a deep sense of spiritual judgment. Which, of course, was self-generated fear, but no less real for being that. My tongue was stoppered because of these feelings, and my walk was hampered. What young Christian can grow without true and transparent guidance from his elders in the Faith?

The answer—you can't.

A Christian will lack depth, confidence, and strength without complete confession and acceptance. We need to know our struggles are shared, and that those struggles don't invalidate us as believers. I want to tell you how this glorious acceptance came to me.

Thirteen years ago, I was outside (on the yard, as we say in prison) playing pickleball. Pickleball is an awesome game that displays the greatest of athletics … okay, it's a semi-athletic game of meagre ability, but it's fun. That's beside the point. Anyway, my opponent and I got into a disagreement about a ridiculous line call. Heated words were exchanged where he called me a "Bible-thumping" curse word, and I reacted physically. It was a bad day for me, thankfully one that has not been repeated.

As a young Christian, I was crushed. I'd thought I was "above" all that. Fighting? Me? It made me feel so low. Was this the real me? These battered fists? Then I started to think about confessing this episode to my mentors. How would these paragons of virtue react to knowing I had slipped up? To put it lightly, I was terrified and ashamed. I also knew I had to confess it to them because the Bible guides us into that.

So, I called my aunt and told her what happened. I cried and beat myself up, feeling like a failure. She was silent while she listened, and then, she was consoling afterwards, but inside myself I felt so low. Here I was confessing something so base as violence to one who, to my mind, never struggled. They say the "cover-up is worse than the crime," but equally true is "the confession feels worse than the crime." We ended the call with my aunt telling me she'd come to visit soon.

She came to visit soon after with her husband. They listened as I told them what happened in all its inglorious detail. When I was finished speaking, I expected some verbal consolation that would leave me feeling worse than I already felt. Instead, my aunt looked at me and asked, "Have you confessed this to God?" To which I answered in the affirmative. She then said, "Well, that's over, then. So how was church this week?"

I was floored. No judgment, no consolation? To wreck my paradigm even more, my uncle said, "I'd have punched him too," and my aunt agreed. What! Did they just say that?

Seeing my incredulous look, my aunt and uncle said something along the lines of us being human and all of us falling short. They told me that my anger was legit, and it was just the execution that failed, which could happen to any of us. It probably already had. I can't tell you how this freed me from bondage, a bondage made up of self-contained and self-imposed feelings of inadequacy. To know that it was okay and normal to feel these things was liberating. More than that, to know that others, especially those further in their walk, dealt with these things was groundbreaking.

Which left me feeling motivated. I wanted to talk about all the hidden doubt, fear, and anger with other believers. I couldn't be the only one battling these things and feeling spiritually restrained from doing so. If only we could talk to each other openly about them and come to realize that we all struggle. It's one thing to know in theory that "All have sinned and fallen short of the glory of God." It's another thing to open the discussion among believers about exactly how each of us experiences those things.

Plus, we don't have to stop at just sin. Let's talk about fear, hate, revenge, love, forgiveness, and truth. What do they mean, what do they look like, and can they actually deepen our faith and not demean it? I believe so. I believe a person's walk will encounter all these things, and it's better to start these discussions now than when we're knee-deep in the struggle.

These beliefs and experiences drive *Mourning Into Dancing*. They are what I hoped to accomplish. I pray God will use this book to bless lives and shift paradigms, as mine was shifted thirteen years ago in a prison visiting room.

I want to thank all the people who believed in God's plan for my life. Your steadfast dedication to faith in a beleaguered saint gave me strength when my own was failing. Thank you to every reader who picked up this book and went on this journey with me. I pray that God blesses you all, and that Jesus Christ walks by your side.

Standing tall,
Aaron Pettes
December 2021

ABOUT THE AUTHOR

Aaron Pettes is recklessly and unashamedly in love with Jesus Christ. At the age of forty-one, he wrote *Riverside Epiphany* (his first work), drawn and embellished from his checkered past. Currently residing in the Federal Bureau of Prisons in Greenville, Illinois, Aaron pursues his dream of writing and creation with the same fervor he employed during his life on the streets. With only three years until his release, he continues to follow God, find his voice, and produce fruit in accordance with repentance.

RIVERSIDE
EPIPHANY

AARON
PETTES

PROLOGUE

DECEMBER 7

The air in the car was stifling. He cracked a window to let a cool breeze blow into the automobile and onto his face. He did not know if the car was actually that hot or if the heat came from his boiling rage. About thirty yards to his right, the Missouri River glistened like an oily snake in the moonlight. Soon he would plunge the car into the water and sink it to the bottom. Who knows, they might not find it for a few weeks. Maybe never, if he was lucky.

"Almost there." The voice startled Lincoln.

"I know. Thanks, man," he said to his friend, David Manz, who drove the car. David acknowledged him with a head nod. Lincoln was thankful for David's silent demeanor. He needed time to think.

There was the sound again, the muffled cries and thumps of the cargo in the trunk. He hoped maybe the traitor had tired himself out and become resigned to his fate, but he'd been wrong. The cries and bumps grew more urgent as the car slowed. Soon there would be only silence from the trunk, but first Lincoln needed to see the man's face just once more. He needed to look the traitor in the eye before he sank into the Missouri, entombed in his own silver Mercedes.

"Point the nose toward the river," Lincoln told David. "I don't want the car to get hung up on anything."

"Okay," said the man of few words.

Lincoln looked in the rearview mirror and saw Li'l Al still following behind in his charcoal Escalade, lights doused, driving only by the beams of his parking lights. They all knew this patch of land well enough to drive there blindfolded.

David pulled the car to a stop at the top of a steep slope that fell twenty feet down to the river. He cut the engine, left the keys in the ignition, and got out of the car, leaving Lincoln in the passenger seat with only his thoughts. After a moment, Lincoln leaned over and rolled all the windows down. He stepped out of the car—now a silver metal casket—and into the night.

The trailing Escalade pulled to a stop directly behind the Mercedes. Li'l Al jumped out of the SUV and walked over to where his friends stood, both of them looking at the rear end of the Benz. Nobody spoke. The only noise was the man struggling inside the trunk.

"Sink the mother—" Li'l Al began to say, but Linc cut him off.

"I need to see his face." Linc's tone killed any argument from his friend and cousin.

Lincoln stepped forward and reached for the latch on the trunk of the car. The hood came up to reveal a bound, blindfolded, gagged man struggling against his bonds. Lincoln reached in and ripped the duct tape off the man's eyes and mouth. The man spit out the dirty gym sock gag and vomited all over himself. He squinted up into the trunk light's glare, trying to make out his abductors.

"Do you know who I—" he shouted, but choked off his outrage when he saw Lincoln's face. The man stuttered, trying to find words.

Lincoln spat into his face. "For Safina."

Two words. Who would have thought two words could make a grown man cry? The man in the trunk cried, babbled, blubbered. Lincoln slammed the lid shut just before the man began to beg. Begging could not—would not—save him.

RIVERSIDE EPIPHANY

Lincoln walked slowly around the car, ignoring the screams from the trunk, and reached in to start the engine. He grabbed the section of two-by-four they'd brought along and wedged it down on the gas pedal. The engine roared. He put the car in gear, and it shot down the embankment and straight into the river. The car's impact into the water jarred the two-by-four loose, and the engine went silent. The only sound was the slow wash-and-gurgle of the car filling up and the screams from the doomed man in the trunk.

As the car slowly sank, Lincoln's anger and despair pushed its way to the surface. He had only been out of prison for three days and here he was, watching a man die. Although he would almost surely escape legal justice for the murder, he could feel the dead man's weight on his shoulders. The lower the car sank, the lower he did, until he was on his knees, tears streaming down his cheeks. His friends stood behind him. They knew this was his decision to make, and his decision would be good enough for them.

The trunk was only a few inches from being fully submerged. The cries for mercy still emanated from the car.

"Mercy!" Lincoln whispered into the darkness. "How about justice? Can you say that, you bastard?"

Why, God? Where are you? How could you let me do this? I thought you'd be by my side, by my family's, to protect us. I did my part. He prayed desperately. *Where are you? Answer me!*

He put his hand into his pocket as he watched the trunk disappear below the surface.

CHAPTER ONE

He woke to the sounds and smells of breakfast—the soft clink of eggs being beaten with a wire whisk, the quiet sizzle of bacon frying, and the comforting aroma of pancakes cooling on the counter. Not a bad start to any day, but especially good after pulling an all-nighter involving belly-crawling over wet grass, bypassing an intense alarm code, cracking a safe, and making a clean getaway.

That had been Lincoln Charles Jr.'s night and his life for the last ten years. Most would correctly call his vocation burglary. He called it "relieving the rich of their burdensome wealth." But last night had been his last heist. He now had enough money to retire quietly, raise his family, and not have to worry about college tuitions, daycare, or anything else. He had been telling himself for years, *you got to know when the time comes to say "Enough." Otherwise, you end up in prison*. Now was the time for him. He was out.

As he stared at the ceiling, Lincoln Charles Jr. thought about the last ten years and how he had come to be where he was now. He'd been born in 1988 in Omaha, Nebraska. His mother, a middle-class suburban white girl, had met his very much older and very much blacker dad at a stoplight one day in 1987. The way the story went, Mom had apparently cut Dad off in traffic. When Dad got out to explain the intricacies of driving in no uncertain terms, he caught one look at the princess behind the wheel and fell for her hard and fast.

Mom was not so enthralled. Dad did several months of wooing before he made any ground, but eventually he was rewarded. They dated for a few months before they eloped to Vegas. They were married for fourteen blissful years until Dad was killed in what police said was a random shooting. Nobody was ever arrested.

Lincoln's mom had witnessed the murder but never said anything to the police. If she'd talked, she would have had to reveal too much, and then she might have ended up in jail along with the killer. Her husband had been a professional criminal who made his living on life's darker side. The man who killed him, a partner who'd cheated him on a job, had murdered Lincoln's dad in an effort to dodge payment.

Two years later, heartbroken but carrying on for the sake of her only son and husband's namesake, Judith Charles got her revenge. She actually ran into Jason Digby, the killer, at a store, and he'd hit on her. She batted her eyes and feigned adoration, agreeing to a date. They met at a hotel. and when Digby opened the door, expecting a night of unfettered intimacy, he received a blast to the face from a .45 caliber handgun. Judith Charles, former head cheerleader and suburban priss, had killed a man. And somehow she got away with it.

Lincoln had been about eleven at the time. He remembered waking up to hear his mom sobbing in her room. He had crept down the hallway and slowly approached her. She sat on the edge of her bed, shoulders shaking. She still had the gun in her hands. "Momma," he whispered quietly. "What happened?"

She had looked at him with wide eyes. Almost to herself, she said, "Lincoln? Everything's okay. Don't worry. I got him."

"Who, Momma?"

"The man who took your daddy," she answered, and went back to crying into her hands.

Lincoln had stood there stunned at the idea of his mother having killed somebody. But the same somebody had taken his father from him.

"Good," he whispered.

"Huh?"

"Nothing, Momma. Here, gimme that." He took the gun from her, ran out into the back yard, and buried the gun under a tree. He came back inside, pulled his mom's coat off, and made her crawl into bed. She was still crying, so he crawled in next to her and held her. Then he started to cry too, and they fell asleep, but not before he whispered once more, "I'm glad he's dead!"

The next morning they got up and went on with their lives, never speaking again about the incident. Lincoln became the man of the house and did a great job. Mom worked long hours, but every night they had dinner together and talked about Dad. They had only each other to talk to, as his mom's family had disowned her for marrying a black man, and his dad's family were all dead but one. A single uncle remained, but he was in prison. He had not been around for a few years, but Uncle Kirkland was a good man and kind to Lincoln.

As Lincoln grew into a young man, he got the reputation around his neighborhood for being a brawler. He was no big kid, but Lincoln Charles had the primal instinct to win. His mother had seen this, and she enrolled him in boxing to try to bring some order to her son's life. And boxing had worked, to a certain extent. He learned control, and he learned to use his head and his wits first. He won numerous titles as a teenager, and a mystique followed him. You did not mess with Lincoln Charles Jr. Not unless you wanted your teeth knocked out.

When Lincoln was fourteen, Uncle Kirkland got out of prison. That day was one of the happiest days of Lincoln's life, and it also began his introduction and instruction into a life of crime. He had come home from school to find his mother and uncle laughing and carrying on in their living room.

"Hey, boy!" Kirkland had laughed, prying himself from the young man's grip. "Look at you! You gotta be what, five foot ten?"

"Five nine and a half and still growing." Lincoln proudly stood up straight, trying to stretch every inch.

"Yeah, you're gonna be tall, just like your daddy. But can you throw a punch?" Putting up one of his hands, he invited Lincoln to give him his best shot. Lincoln smiled shyly, then struck like a cobra. *Whack!*

"Dang, boy!" Kirkland said loudly, as he rubbed his hand. "What you got this kid eating, Judith?"

"I'm the only girl in here, Kirk," Judith chided. "Stop crying, you'll embarrass yourself!"

"Yeah, I'll show you who's a girl!" He scooped Lincoln onto his shoulders and dumped him on the couch. They all shared in a laugh.

Later on, after dinner, Lincoln found his uncle on the back porch smoking a cigarette and staring silently into the night sky.

"You miss Dad too?" he asked.

"He was my best friend, Lincoln. I miss him every day."

"Teach me to be like Dad was," Lincoln asked, in almost a begging tone.

"Your dad was a—how should I say—a criminal entrepreneur. I don't know if that's what you or your mom want for your life." He stopped staring into the night and brought his gaze to bear on his nephew. "Do you know what you're asking, son?"

"I know who Dad was. I ain't stupid. He showed me how to pick the lock on the cookie cabinet, didn't he?" Lincoln said, with no small amount of pride.

"Well, we're not talking about cookies, are we?"

"Either you teach me, or I'll do it my way. It can't be too hard."

"Boy, there are rules you have to follow in the business. Things you gotta know, or you could end up dead. This is not a game," his uncle said, frowning.

"That's why I need your help." Now Lincoln begged in earnest.

"You're only thirteen—"

"I'm fourteen! And I'll be fifteen soon!"

Silence settled over the night as uncle and nephew squared off, neither wanting to give in. Kirkland could see his brother's determination in the boy's eyes, along with something close to desperation. Could he bring his brother's son into this life? The boy's stance gave him his answer. Lincoln would make things happen, with or without him.

"It's okay, Kirkland."

They both jumped, startled, and saw Judith Charles looking at them through the screen door. She stepped out into the night, grabbed her brother-in-law's hand, and looked up into his face. "It's okay, if that's what he wants. I'd rather have you there showing him the ropes."

Kirkland looked down at her, this woman beloved by his brother, and he was amazed by her strength. No wonder his brother had been drawn in by her. The intensity of her gaze showed her resolve. Neither she nor his nephew knew of the past he and his brother had shared or the pact they had made. They had agreed if one brother died, the other was to step in and take care of the family left behind. To honor the pact with his brother, he would protect this woman with all he had, and he would teach the boy what he knew.

"Okay. We'll start soon."

After that, whenever there was free time, Uncle Kirkland would pick Lincoln up and take him over to his home. They would spend hours in the "workshop"—the name Lincoln gave his uncle's basement—where he was schooled in everything from safe cracking, surveillance, electronics, and the subterfuge needed to think fast on his feet and be a good actor.

"Never resort to violence. Never," his uncle instructed. "This is the most important rule of all."

"But what if someone comes home? Or doesn't want to give up their money?"

"If someone comes home, you bail. And we aren't robbers, Lincoln. We don't hurt people." His uncle drew close to him. "We hit when no one's home, or we do our work right under their noses, but we do not resort to violence. Do you understand me?"

"Yes, sir."

"Make sure you do. Your dad was no killer, remember that."

"I will. I promise."

"I believe you, son."

The lessons continued, and the rules continued. No taking from people who have less. Always have a good, solid partner. Never rush a job—take time and do the job right. And on and on until the rules were ingrained into Lincoln's mind. Lincoln remembered those years with great fondness, the spending of those endless hours next to a man who loved him and reminded him so much of his dad. His uncle's wife—Kim Li, a small Korean woman his uncle had met and fallen in love with during his time in the army—would bring them dinners while they worked. Lincoln would use those times to pepper his uncle with questions, trying to absorb everything the man knew.

"Ask questions, Linc. Listen and store everything away," his uncle encouraged. "Your father would be proud."

Lincoln had eventually partnered with his cousin Li'l Al, Kirkland's son. They called him Li'l Al because of his obvious height disadvantage. Being of mixed race had doomed him. His Asian heritage claimed dominance, and Alyas Charles, aka Li'l Al, never grew past five foot five in height. Several years into their partnership, Li'l Al's "career" ended when he got into a serious car accident and shattered his right leg. He ended up with a serious limp, and that was that.

When Li'l Al retired, he and Lincoln went fifty-fifty and opened a club on the Westside of Omaha. They named the club Potential, and it quickly became the hottest spot in town. Lines of young men and women were the regulars at

Potential. They hired all their boys in the neighborhood as bouncers and bartenders, always keeping their circle tight. Lincoln Charles was the unspoken leader of their crew.

After his cousin's medical leave, Linc partnered with an old friend, Clinton Wills. Clint Wills was nowhere near as good as Li'l Al, but he handled his business. He was a little impetuous, wanting to rush things, but Lincoln had the ability to rein him in. They'd made a good partnership for two years, until the day Lincoln had decided to retire. Last night.

The conversation had been a little tense, but tension was to be expected. They were raking in cash, and the operation had always run smoothly with both of them there.

"Come on, man," Clinton had said. "The money is flowing. Why break up a good thing?"

"I'm not denying it's good, my man," Lincoln explained. "But you know Safina is pregnant. I want to be around to raise my family."

"I hear you, but come on. We're ahead, and—"

"Perfect time to quit, Clint." Lincoln cut off his friend. "Don't worry. You can keep the tools, the client list, all of it. Find yourself a new partner, and you'll be fine. You got the skills."

"Yeah, I know, man, but you are the best. This is a little hard for me to believe. At the pinnacle of success, you're quitting. I don't like it, Linc, is all." Clinton grudgingly let it go.

Well, it doesn't matter if you like it. It's over after tonight.

Lying in his bed the next morning, Lincoln prepared to enjoy the first-day fruits of his retirement. He sat up, wiped the crud from his eyes, and padded into his bathroom. He used the toilet, brushed his teeth, and called out to his fiancée.

"Safina!"

CHAPTER TWO

Maplewood Village was a nice middle-class neighborhood in the northwest part of Omaha, Nebraska. Comprised mostly of two-bedroom and three-bedroom homes, small yards, a lot of tall trees, kids on bikes, and dogs behind fences eager to please, Maplewood was an all-around cozy place to live. Small to nonexistent gangs, low crime rate, block parties for the residents, yet not a gossip prone area. The neighborhood was a place where everyone still lived their own lives.

Maplewood was also a perfect place for a lowkey criminal entrepreneur to blend in and be accepted warmly by his fellow citizens. As long as business stayed away from home, which it always did, a man could live comfortably away from the eye of the law. Lincoln was a good neighbor, grilling out occasionally, throwing Super Bowl parties, and passing himself off as a work-from-home computer guru, buying and selling on websites—vague business activities no one questioned.

His home was a three-bedroom house, no better or worse than the rest on his block. He kept his lawn manicured in the summer, sidewalks shoveled in the winter. He owned two cars, actually one car and one minivan, which he had just traded for because of the baby expected in the near future. His car was the only real flash he owned, a forest-green Ford Mustang on 22-inch chrome wheels with black wall tires, metallic paint, tinted windows, black-on-green interior, and a stereo system to take your breath away. No heavy bass, though—too much. The ride was extra low, and from the front, when it moved, the car seemed to hover.

Lincoln was comfortable and content. He had just reached his goal of two million in savings and was confident he could live easy for a lifetime. Maybe do a little investing now and then. Nothing outrageous, just enough to supplement his lifestyle. Plus, he maintained half ownership in the hottest club in Omaha. Club Potential was still a very lucrative business and would definitely boost his savings over the years.

Now was the perfect time to retire. He was twenty-five years old with a fiancée who was four months pregnant, and no arrests marred his past. Yes, there was one hothead detective, one Detective Danny O'Brien of the Omaha Police Department, but O'Brien had nothing on him. Nothing except a strong, and albeit legit, suspicion that Lincoln Charles was the head of the most prolific burglary ring in Omaha's history. But he would not have to worry about Detective O'Brien any longer, because he was finally out.

Now, standing in his bathroom with a mouthful of Listerine, he allowed himself a moment of self-congratulation. He chuckled and spit into the sink, shut off the water, and walked back into his bedroom. He dressed in a tank top and sweatpants and made his way downstairs. On the way, he stopped by the room next to his. He had just finished turning what was his game room into a nursery. Gone were the leather couch, big screen TV, and PlayStation 4. In their places sat a crib, playpen, other baby paraphernalia, and the walls were painted soft lavender with sappy bunnies and butterflies. Safina's doing, of course.

He took a deep breath, considering his situation. Soon he would be a father and a husband. He hoped he had the gumption to do well at those jobs. He was a great thief—meticulous, patient, cool-headed, dedicated—and he hoped he could draw from those skills and succeed. *Every father had those worries, and he was no different*. Well, sort of.

RIVERSIDE EPIPHANY

Continuing down the hall and down the five steps into his living room, he made his way to the kitchen and the source of the attractive smells. The radio on the counter was on the local old-school, hip-hop station, and the sounds were mixing with the melody of his fiancée singing along. And there she stood, the girl of his dreams, in a pair of tiny boxers and tank top, her baby bump visible between the tops of the boxers and the bottom of the tank top. She was doing her best approximation of shaking her tailfeather while pouring a glass of orange juice. *This was heaven.*

He strode up behind her and caught her mid-wiggle. She jumped a little and sloshed a little juice on the counter.

"Baby!" she said in surprise, as his arms enveloped her. "Well, good morning to you too."

"You are the most amazing creature," Lincoln said, as he pulled her close, their bodies melting together. "You couldn't be more alluring than you are right now."

Turning around and kissing him softly on his lips, she whispered, "You're not so shabby yourself, my love."

"Yeah, I know," he replied, with a smug smile.

"And there you go." She pulled away from him. "You couldn't stay humble, could you?"

"What am I supposed to do, deny the truth?" he said in mock astonishment. "Look at this physique, this dimple. Come on."

"You're silly." She eased back into his grasp. "I don't know why I put up with you."

"I do."

"And why is that?"

"Because I am hopelessly in love with you," he growled.

"Yes, you're right," she purred back, as they softly kissed. "So, are you ready for breakfast? I made the works."

"I see," Lincoln said, taking in the cornucopia of food on the kitchen table. "You still haven't gotten over your cravings."

"Hey, no poking fun at the pregnant fiancée," she said, as she displayed her lovely figure. "Besides, I still got my shape, for however long it lasts."

Patting her small bottom, Lincoln agreed. "Yeah, I have to agree with you. Let's eat, babe."

They sat down to eat as Justin Timberlake played from the radio. His mouth full of pancakes, Lincoln stared across the table at his fiancée. Safina Raines, twenty-three years old, of Irish descent. Alabaster skin, green eyes, dark reddish-brown hair, petite build, about five-foot-six and a hundred and ten pounds. She was not knockout gorgeous, but she was definitely a pretty girl with a certain spark that would draw any man. And what a spark she was—witty, smart, strong, yet soft at the same time. A woman. Her ability to match Lincoln's verbal prowess in debates was what had caught his attention at first. A recent graduate from UNL, the state university, she was as book smart as she was street smart.

Lincoln had met her at Potential after they had closed one night. He and his boys hung around playing cards, talking trash, and trading ideas. She had been there with a few of the girls who were waitresses. While they finished their jobs, she migrated over to where Lincoln and his boys were debating whether women were better liars than men.

"Seriously, James, you can't really believe that." Lincoln was trying to nail down his friend's position.

"I do," James had responded with a grin. "Men are better than women at most things, and this is no different."

"I know a few women who'd disagree," Lincoln countered. "Women have something we men absolutely cannot compete with, my friend. Curious?"

"Enlighten me, Linc." James's words dripped with sarcasm.

Lincoln had caught Safina's eye and invited her into the conversation. "Do me a favor, would ya?" he asked. "How old are you?"

196

"Twenty-one," she had answered, curious.

They all looked back at James, who was caught staring at Safina's bosom. Everyone burst out laughing.

"See? That's what I'm talking about." Linc crowed his delight at his friend's easy defeat. "Women have weapons to stun men into silence and leave them open to any deception. We can't compete with such weapons."

"So, are you saying all women are liars?" Safina jumped back in defiantly, apparently a little miffed.

Lincoln immediately backpedaled. "No, not at all. See, we're only discussing who was better. I wasn't implying all women lie or are liars."

There was a little tension now, so Lincoln stood up and offered his hand. "I'm sorry if I offended you. I'm Lincoln Charles, Junior. And you are ...?"

She answered with a spark in her eyes and a smirk on her face. "My name is Safina." She took his hand. "And I'm twenty-two."

Everyone burst out laughing again, but this time at Linc for being beaten at his own game. Even he had to laugh at the trap he'd set for himself and the grace with which this woman had fooled him.

"Twenty-two, huh? See, fellas, happens to the best of us." Still holding her hand. "Join us, please."

And she had sat down and never got up. Eighteen months later, she sat across from him ready to be his wife. The wedding was scheduled for December, a little more than three months away. He considered himself to be the luckiest man in Omaha.

She caught him smiling at her, and through a mouthful of eggs, she said, "What? Do I have something in my teeth?"

He chuckled. "No, just considering how lucky I am."

"I know. I've been saying it for months."

"Now who's prideful?" he said, as he threw a piece of bacon at her, hitting her right on the forehead.

A handful of eggs flew over Lincoln's head, just as the phone rang. Lincoln ducked, laughing, and got up to answer the ring.

"Don't worry, I'll get it!" He picked up the phone, still laughing. "Hello?"

"Linc, hey, man, it's me," the voice said.

A pancake hit Lincoln in the face. "You're gonna pay for that, woman. I swear!" Safina giggled in the background.

"What? Who, me?" the voice on the phone asked.

"Nah, man, not you. I got a half-crazed pregnant woman sitting at my kitchen table launching breakfast projectiles at me. But anyways, what's up, Clint?"

"I need to talk to you. I'm outside in the driveway. You got a second?"

"Yeah, man. I'll be out in a minute." He hung up. "You're on cleanup duty, girl."

"I don't think so!" she said, grabbing her plate and dashing up the stairs. "You're right where you belong, barefoot and in the kitchen!"

"We'll see 'bout that!" he hollered to her. "Hey, I'll be right back. Clint's outside and needs to talk."

He got no reply, but he knew she had heard. He headed to the front door, put on a jacket and shoes, and opened the door.

What does this fool want? He wondered as he shut the door behind him.

CHAPTER THREE

Stepping into the mid-morning sunshine, Lincoln turned his face up to the sky just to feel the warmth on his face. In his driveway, Clint sat behind the wheel of a pearlescent white 1985 Chevy Monte Carlo. The car was a beautiful ride with cream leather, chrome trim, and T-tops. Clint sat behind the wheel, bobbing his head to Tupac Shakur's "Dear Mama," an old-school song in an old-school ride. If you saw Clint outside his car you would think he was a stoner or maybe a punk rocker. White dude, skinny, five-nine or so, long hair in a ponytail, baggy clothes. What you would not think was professional burglar with a mean streak. He had started out as a white boy wannabe, but he'd evolved and accepted his whiteness while staying a thug at heart. Not a bad dude, really. He definitely was unique.

Linc got into the passenger side just as the song was coming to an end. Clint reached over and turned the music down.

"So, what's up, man? How's the retirement?" Clint asked.

"I don't know. I haven't had time to enjoy it yet." He remembered the food fight. "I think I'm gonna like it, though."

"Good for you, my friend." Sounding sincere. "If anybody deserves some peace and quiet it's people like us with the lifestyle we lead, ya know?"

"What, Clint? You considering taking a sabbatical?" Linc asked, surprised. "Last night you didn't sound too enthused by my decision."

"Nah, man, you just caught me off guard is all. I didn't mean no disrespect or nothin'. I was just sayin', here we are rollin' in the jobs, and you up and quit. No warning? I mean, again, it's cool, you just surprised me." He paused a breath. "See, it got me thinking too. Ya know? How long do I want to do this? Could I quit? I don't know, man. I think I enjoy the life too much."

Lincoln had never seen this from his gung-ho partner. Maybe he was just talking, but Linc felt the need to speak up. "You have to quit sometime, bro. Let's face it, this is not a job you can do all your life. It's good to have an outlook. A long-term plan."

"I hear you, Linc, and I agree. I do." He looked over at his partner and continued. "Which is why I'm here. I want to run my retirement plan by you, see what you think."

"Okay, man, whatever." Lincoln was getting wary now. Where was this heart-to-heart conversation heading? "You talk. I'm listening."

"So, I go home last night after we finish working. I call up Suzy from Potential—you know, the petite blonde? Anyway, I'm feeling a little juiced still, so I figure some lady company would help get the fuzz out. Well, she comes over, and we commune in the biblical sense. After we're laying there, out of the blue, she says, 'I know what you do for a living.' Kinda catches me off guard, so I'm like 'Yeah, ya think?' She goes, 'You're a thief.'"

"How does she know that?" Lincoln cut in.

"I don't know, but I deny being a thief, of course. She says, 'Yeah, whatever. But I bet if I told you I could put you on a million-dollar score, you'd be a thief then.' We're quiet for a while, my wheels turning. I roll over and ask her, 'Million bucks?' She says, 'Told you.' She goes on to tell me about her boyfriend who beats her and how she left him a few weeks ago. Well, this boyfriend is rolling in green, Linc. She's seen two safes in his closet, one for his guns and one for his cash and jewelry. I ask her if she knows the combos, she says no, but get this, she knows the house alarm code. Gives me the code right there. I ask her how I am supposed to trust the info, she looks at me and says, 'Make the jerk pay for touchin' me.' And I know she's legit by the look in her eyes. She goes on to tell me he's out of town now on business and won't be back 'til tomorrow. Over a million bucks, Linc."

"Well, sounds like you got your nest egg," Lincoln responded. He was definitely intrigued by the story, but he was retired.

"Absolutely, but there's a catch."

"Of course there is." He should have seen it coming.

"The safes are Huhm 3000s. Both of them."

Lincoln whistled his appreciation for the quality of safe this boyfriend had invested in. Top of the line, almost vaults, probably cost at least five thousand each. There were only two people in Omaha who could crack that kind of safe. One was his cousin, Li'l Al, who was out of the business. The other, of course, was him. Now everything made sense.

"So what are you askin', Clint?" He wanted, needed, to hear it from his friend.

"I'm sorry." He wasn't. "I know you're done. You're out and I respect that." He didn't, or else he wouldn't be here. "But I'm talking a fifty-fifty split of a million or more. Five hundred K. Shoot, man, I might join you in retirement with that kind of dough."

"I'm retired," Lincoln said, not sounding too sure. "Five hundred K ..."

"This is solid, Linc, on the level, but we have to move tonight if we are going to do this." Clint saw he had his friend thinking. "I'll give you my word—after this I won't even hint at you about doing no job."

Lincoln sat in thought, running the number around his head. He was not intimidated by the safes. Two hours apiece and they would fall like Goliath under David's sling. But what would Safina say? She was going to be very upset. He had promised her he was done. Their conversation was not going to be a good one at all. But for that kind of money, he could bear the brunt of her anger. He would take her on a shopping spree or on a cruise before she got too big. He did not like rushing jobs, but knowing the alarm code changed things.

Looking over at his friend he made his decision. "Okay, Clint, you got me."

"Yes!" His partner slapped his leg in excitement. "My man! I swear, Linc, you ain't gonna regret this. A million bucks!" He continued talking rapidly in his pleasure of the moment.

"Be here tonight at eleven," Lincoln cut in. "Bring the tools and drive the throwaway, just in case."

"Of course, I know the deal." Clint started the car. "Go back inside and do the domestic thing. Don't let me keep you."

"Eleven." Lincoln got out and made his way inside his house. He took a breath before he opened the door. This was not going to be pretty. He walked in.

Later that night, he stood in his bedroom, getting dressed in his "work uniform." Black combat boots, black military-style cargo pants, long-sleeve tight-fitting cotton shirt. Over that went a black jacket with no pockets, black watchman's cap, and black nylon gloves. He double checked his pockets—all empty. He walked down the hall and saw Safina curled up in the La-Z-Boy, still sulking. He could not blame her though, remembering their confrontation earlier in the morning.

"What? Am I hearing what I think I'm hearing?" Safina was livid. "You said you were out. Now what? You're not?"

"Baby," Lincoln had pleaded. "I'm out, but this is five hundred K we're talkin' about."

The number did not give her any pause. "I don't care, Lincoln. For five hundred million, I still wouldn't care."

He believed her. "I swear."

"You already swore, remember?" she shot back.

Lincoln's anger warmed. "Listen, woman. I run this show. You're my fiancée. I provide for this family, and I can't pass on this."

"Oh, don't give me any bull macho crap. You're getting greedy here, my love, can't you see?" She was right. "I don't care about money. I want you here for me and this baby." She started to cry. Lincoln tried to approach her, but she stepped out of his reach.

"Okay, I feel you, Saffy." His pet name for her. He broke it out when he needed to. "But—"

"No buts, and calling me Saffy isn't going to work."

Well, so much for sweet talk. "Okay, Safina, I don't want you to be mad, but …" He grimaced. "This is happening."

"Oohh!" she said in frustration and flounced off to the bedroom and slammed the door.

Well, things could have been worse. At least she did not throw anything. Her Irish blood ran hot.

He descended the stairs and approached the recliner, pausing before reaching her. The time was 10:59, and Clint would be there soon. He wanted to talk to her before he left, but was unsure. He did not want another fight. He had to be as focused as possible for this job. He started to turn around.

"Lincoln?" Safina peeked over the recliner.

"Oh, God." Lincoln said in relief. He went and knelt by the recliner and put his head on Safina's chest. She wrapped her arms around him. "I thought you were still mad."

"I'm scared, Linc," she said in his ear. "I don't want to lose you."

He looked up into her face. "Baby, you have my heart in your hands. I am yours 'til I breathe my last."

"I know, but ..." She tried to get the words out. "I have a bad feeling on this one."

"I always come back, don't I?"

"Yeah, but—"

"No buts, remember?" he said in an attempt to lighten the mood. "Look at me."

She did.

"I'm comin' home." His tone carried both reassurance and finality.

Clint's car horn sounded in the driveway. Lincoln did not budge. He needed to know his queen was with him.

"Saffy?"

"Come home to me." She kissed his lips. "Now go."

"That's my girl." He stood. "I'll be back," he said, in his best Schwarzenegger imitation, getting a smile out of her. He kissed her again and went to the door, where he saw Clint waiting in the throwaway car.

"This should be easy." And he was gone.

Safina watched him go, and began to cry.

Lincoln got into the throwaway car, its interior ink-dark. A throwaway car is a stolen car, untraceable back to the people using the car if it gets ditched. The dash and overhead lights were all shorted out to avoid any illumination in the car. There would be no possibility of their faces being visible to passing motorists. The car was a dark blue 1997 Dodge Neon, a boring, nondescript model. Lincoln looked in the back and saw all his tools on the seat.

"Cool, man," he said to Clint. "Where we headed?"

"Regency, where else?" Regency was one of the most upscale neighborhoods in Omaha, with all of the houses in the five-hundred-thousand to million-dollar price range. This news pleased Lincoln.

"Ol' boy is out of town 'til when, tomorrow?"

"At least noon," Clint said. "I called the airport, and his plane doesn't get in 'til 11:30 a.m."

"Plenty of time," Linc said, thinking about the time he would need to crack the Huhms.

"Yep."

They rode the rest of the way in silence, adrenaline already pumping in their veins. For Lincoln the silence crystallized his thoughts, bringing them into sharp focus. He lowered his head, visualizing the mechanics of the job ahead. They pulled into the neighborhood and crept up to the house, cutting the headlights.

"I drove by earlier today," Clint told Linc. "We can pull around back. The driveway goes all the way around."

"Cool. Do it."

They pulled around to the back of the house. Clint cut the engine, and they got out. They took empty backpacks from the back seat and put them on. Lincoln gathered his tools while Clinton approached the back door.

Clint knelt at the lock, examined it briefly, and commenced picking it. A minute later, the door swung open, and they closed it behind them as the alarm started to beep its warning. They had only a few seconds to enter the code. Clint went to the keypad, consulted the numbers on his hand.

"Six-four-seven-three," he whispered, and punched them in. The light on the box flashed to green, and the beeping stopped.

"See, brother, easy as pie." He grinned up at Lincoln in the dark.

They knew the safes were in the master bedroom closet. They paid no attention to the house's high-tech electronics as they made their way upstairs. They had to check four rooms before they found the master suite. The room's square footage was easily what Lincoln's first floor of his house had. "Nice to be rich," he whispered into the darkness.

"I hear you, my man," Clint agreed. "Over here."

They found the closet and swung the doors open. The two

safes hulked against the back wall, seeming to dare Lincoln to break them.

"Give me a few hours." *Challenge accepted.* "Keep watch."

"Gotcha." Clinton took up a position by the window while Lincoln opened his bag and went to work. Two grueling hours later, the first safe gave up the fight. With a soft *dink*, the door clicked open.

"Psst." Linc alerted Clint. "One down."

His partner approached. "The legend of Lincoln Charles Junior continues to grow." The doors swung open, revealing a host of handguns, ranging from .22s to .380s, with a few 357s, a 9-millimeter, two .40s, and four .44s. Fifteen total. On the bottom rung of the safe were black cylinders. "Shoot, man, those are silencers!" Clint's excitement was palpable.

"Load 'em up while I start on this second one," Lincoln instructed his partner. Clinton rummaged for a moment in the closet, came up with a duffel bag, and got to work.

Two hours later, *click!*

"Bingo!" Lincoln muttered. "Give up your dreams, my lady!" He sweet talked the safe as he swung open the door and stared. "No way!"

Clint hurried over. "What, man?" But no explanation was needed. The upper of the safe's two shelves held stacks of cash, bundles a foot high, two feet wide, and three feet deep—all hundred-dollar bills.

Lincoln did the math quickly. "Six hundred fifty."

"Grand?"

"Yep."

"Told ya, man. Told ya."

The bottom shelf held two drawers. Lincoln pulled out the first one. It held Rolexes, Bulgari watches, rings crusted with diamonds, cuff links with huge stones. The other drawer held twenty-two one-kilo gold bars, each about the size of a Butterfinger, but considerably heavier.

"Seriously?" Lincoln said in awe.

"Told ya, man. Told ya," Clinton repeated.

"Let's load it up." Linc took off his backpack and started filling it with gold bars and jewelry. "Get the cash."

"Got it." When Clint bent over to start loading the packets of bills, he accidentally hit the wall switch. Light blazed in the dark house.

"Turn it off! Now!" Lincoln flashed angrily.

The light went out. "Dang. My fault."

"Let's go. Load up the cash." They hurried to finish.

Next door, Harold Ramsey stood at his toilet. At age sixty-five, he did more standing than peeing, which gave him an excellent view when the light blazed from the Salvatore residence. His bathroom window looked right at the house. He knew Mr. Salvatore was out of town, because he'd seen him leave last week. Had he come back early? No, because the light went out as fast as it appeared. He put himself away and went to the wall phone to dial 9-1-1.

"I'd like to report suspicious activity," he said into the handset.

As they finished loading the packs, Lincoln noticed a business card. He picked it up and squinted to make out the name.

Vincent Salvatore, Waste Management Consultant.

Vincent Salvatore. Why did the name sound familiar? His memory clicked. Vinny Sal, hitman for the mob. Waste management consultant? Cute.

"Clint, what the—?" Linc whispered to his partner. "Did you know we were robbing Vinny freakin' Sal?"

He better not say yes. But the pause was confirmation.

He grabbed Clint and slammed him against the wall. He held him by the lapels of his coat, his face right next to his partner's. "I should bust your teeth out, you idiot. You're lucky we're pressed for time."

"I knew you'd say no, man," Clinton whined. He struggled to extricate himself from Lincoln's grasp. "Let's go, man."

"Leave the tools and guns," Lincoln said, as he turned to go.

"What? Why?"

"I'm not going to need the tools and the guns. They'll slow us down. We have to move, now."

They fled down the stairs with the packs and got to the car. Lincoln slid in behind the wheel. They crept down the drive, lights out, and pulled onto the street. Rolling down the block, they made the corner and flipped on their lights, just as a police cruiser turned the corner and came toward them.

"Cops," Lincoln warned. "Be cool. Let 'em roll on by."

The police car rolled by and then slowed. Clint made a fatal mistake. He looked back. The cruiser pulled an immediate U-turn and hit its lights. Lincoln jammed the accelerator and sped off. But a 1997 Dodge Neon was no match for a police unit. They screamed around a few corners, but the cruiser kept up with them.

"I'm going to slow down," Lincoln said. "Jump out. We gotta split up."

"Gotcha." Clint did not question him.

Lincoln hit one more corner and slowed to almost a full stop. Clint grabbed one of the bags and sprang from the car. He disappeared as Linc sped off. The cruiser stayed with him.

I need to ditch this car. He took a couple more corners to put extra space between himself and Clinton, and the cruiser fell back. He grabbed the remaining backpack, ready to jump from the car, and immediately regretted his decision. Clint had grabbed the one with the cash, leaving him the one with the jewelry and almost fifty pounds of gold.

The choice of bags wouldn't have mattered. As soon as he hit the pavement, an ultra-bright spotlight from the hovering ghetto bird—police helicopter—lit him up. Three cruisers screeched to a stop. Doors flew open. Guns were drawn.

"Down! Now!"

"Hands! Let us see your hands!"

"Police!"

Lincoln slowly raised his hands, dropping the backpack. The only thought he had was of Safina and his unborn child.